FINESSED BY A SAVAGE

MS. KEENA

Visit Our Website To Sign-up For Our Mailing List
www.UrbanChaptersPublications.com
If you would like to join our team, submit the first 3-4 chapters of your completed manuscript to
Submissions@UrbanChapterspublications.com

Be sure to join our reading group to connect with all authors under Urban Chapters Publications.
www.facebook.com/chillin'with UCP
Text Jahquel to 345345!

Be sure to bless our page with a LIKE!

ACKNOWLEDGMENTS

Thank you, thank you, thank you to everyone that took the time out to purchase this book and all my other books. You guys don't know how nerve-racking it was worrying if you guys would like it.

To my heartbeats, you are a reflection of me, so it's only right that I show you that anything can be accomplished with motivation. I hope that I am the inspiration that you seek when times get tough.

To my love, my best friend, and my biggest supporter, Charles, it only gets better. All the trials and tribulations will finally pay off as long as we stay strong together.

To my readers, thank you for your continued support. You guys gave me the push I needed with the numerous inboxes, comments, and reviews.

To my family, both near and far, thank you for the calls, texts, and support in ordering books. It's because of your support, through word of mouth and sharing posts on Facebook that these books have been a success.

It's by the grace of God that I have continued writing. There have been so many times that I wanted to give up, but I know that I was given a talent that needed to be shared with the world.

Follow me:
Twitter: @Theauthorkeena
Instagram: theauthorkeena
Facebook: Sakina Thomas & Author Keena
Facebook Author Page: Author Keena
Reading Group: Sakina Sensational Readers

1

Kashmir

"How much longer are you going to let Gio keep using you as his doormat?" Starr asked.

I was sitting there listening to Starr and Serenity go on and on about Gio and how he wasn't shit. I mean they weren't saying anything that I wasn't thinking already, but it still hurt to hear them say it. I had just told them that I was confronted by yet another woman claiming to have a child by him. The bitch even knew where I lived and all.

Hi, I'm Kashmir, a 26-year-old Director of Public Relations at one of this most sought after PR firm,by everyone in the entertainment industry. tired of my boyfriend, Gio, and his continuous cheating, pregnancy scares and DNA tests on a monthly basis. It didn't start out like this when we first started dating. He was three years older than me when we first met in college. Once he graduated from school and his best friend got out of prison, everything really started to change. Staying out late or not even coming home at all. Add to that, the countless females calling his phone and texting at all times of the night.

I was devastated when I first found out about Kayla, his daughter's mother. Imagine the look on my face when there was a knock at the door, and there she stood with a baby in her arms. Here I was being the faithful, loyal girlfriend, and he was laying and playing with anything walking. I had my chance with some of the hottest acts walking and believe me I had my share of offer and which I should've taken up a time or to, but I remained loyal. And this was my ending result.

I had milk chocolate complexion with natural hair that hung to the middle of my back. I had thick thighs with a small waist; some would say I was shaped like a coke bottle, and I loved every bit of my curves. I was the director of PR at my firm and worked hard to get that position at such a young age. I cook, cleaned, and made sure I laid it down in the bedroom, but I guess Gio didn't see it that way.

"Hello! Earth to Kash," Serenity said.

"My bad, y'all. What were you saying?" I asked.

"I was saying that you need to get rid of his dog-faced ass. Find you someone that is for you and will be just as good for you," Serenity said.

We had been sitting at our weekend lunch place as we do every weekend my *Momma Red's* soul food restaurant. We all were so busy during the weekday, so this was our day to catch up on each other's lives.

"So what your ass going to do? Continue to be the doormat or nah?" Starr asked.

She was the blunt one and didn't sugar coat anything for anyone. I respected her for that because a lot of so-called friends would get all your information and then talk behind your back to others. Not with Starr, though. She always said, "*If I said it once, I damn sure can say it again.*"

You got to love her for that. Serenity was the one that thought before she spoke to make sure that she wouldn't hurt anyone's feeling. I loved both of them equally and they balanced each other out. Starr was a twenty-nine year old single mother, who was just finishing school to become a Pediatric Nurse. She was also the mom to my God-daughter Amina, who was now four years old. While

Serenity was twenty-eight and a social worker with a 6 year old son. She had also just broke up with her dude because he was a bum.

"Look, all I'm saying is we can go over to your house, pack his shit, change the locks really quick and drop it to his momma house for all I care, just get it up out of yours," Serenity said.

My girls were down for whatever and I loved them for that. They both were older than me by a couple years, but that didn't stop us from hanging out or talking every day.

"Why won't he be faithful, y'all? What's wrong with me?" I asked them.

"Bitch, make me come across this table. There isn't a damn thing wrong with you. That's his lying, sneaky, cheating ass that has the issue," Starr stated.

"Starr's right, there isn't nothing wrong with so you can get that shit out of your brain right now," Serenity chimed in.

Gio had been blowing up my phone, but I hadn't answered his calls since I left the house this morning. Before I met with the girls, I thought about my father, who was the only one that has always been there for me. Even when he and my mother divorced, he still broke his neck to make sure that I didn't want or need for anything. He remarried when I was about ten to Momma Shan, and I loved her to death. She was so sweet, and I was happy when she had my baby brother. My mother, on the other hand, tried everything in her power to keep me away from my father and even tried to turn me against him when Jaylin was born. Telling me that he wouldn't treat me the same, but he never changed anything. In fact, I think he spoiled me more because I was older and his baby girl at the same time. He couldn't stand Gio so when I tell him about the latest drama, he will want to grab my uncles and go break his foot off in his ass.

Snapping back to the conversation that was still going on, I had come to the conclusion that I couldn't continue to be with Gio and that I deserved better than he was giving me.

"I'm breaking up with Gio," I stated.

"Bitch, I know you lying," Starr said.

"I'm for real. I can't keep doing this. Enough is enough."

"Well, let's get going before this bitch change her mind and take the nigga back. Y'all head to the house and start packing his shit, and I'll go get some locks," Starr said.

I jumped into Serenity's car, and we headed towards my house.

"Call that nigga to make sure that he isn't at the house," Serenity said.

I didn't want to hear his voice, so I sent him a text instead like nothing was wrong.

Me: Hey, you home?
Liar: Nah, I just ran off real quick. What's up?
Me: I'll talk to you later about it.
Liar: Ok.

Thank god he isn't home because I sure as hell don't feel like dealing with him. It took us maybe ten minutes to get to my house from the restaurant. As we walked into the house, I could tell that he had left not too long ago because I could still smell his cologne. Walking into the kitchen, I got some trash bags and Serenity and I headed to my bedroom. We began to bag up his clothes, leaving the stuff that I had bought. I be damned if he wears those clothes, shoes and jewelry that I bought for another woman. I would give the clothes and shoes to the needy and the jewelry I would either pawn or give it to my brother.

Starr arrived about ten minutes after we did and went to work changing all of the locks in the house. She even reprogrammed the garage door opener so that he couldn't get in through the garage. I tell you Starr was a beast and didn't play when it came to breaking up with a dude and keeping them out of her house.

It felt surreal. Here I was packing up Gio's stuff and changing locks; never had I imagined that I would be doing this after all the years that we had been together.

"Girl, hurry the hell up!" Starr yelled.

We were loading up Gio's things in Starr's truck to take them to his baby momma Kayla's house. She wanted him so bad she could have him and all his drama because I was done. We put the last of his shit in the truck and headed over to her apartment.

When we pulled up to the apartment complex, there was a couple dudes outside, and the kids was playing.

"Kash, isn't that his car?' Serenity asked.

"Starr, go over to the car under the tree," I said.

As we got closer to the car, I saw hanging on the mirror the VIP pass to the Jay-Z concert I had surprised him for his birthday hanging there.

"Hell yeah that his mother fucking car. Stop and unlock the back door," I said to Starr.

I jumped out of the backseat and started unloading the bags of clothes. Starr and Serenity followed behind me and helped out. I was sick of his ass and was putting all of his clothes on top of his most prized possession- his car. After we finished taking all the bags out, I went back into the truck, pulled out my keys, and started keying the entire car.

"YO! She fucking that car up," One of the dudes said.

"Bitch, flatten those tires too," Starr said, handing me her knife.

I tell you if it was some shit to go down, Starr was the one you wanted to be with you. Taking her knife, I flattened all four of his tires.

"Girl, hurry up before someone call the cops," Serenity said.

Hopping back into the truck, we headed back to my house so that I could grab my car and pack a bag for a couple days. I needed to clear my head and being in the house with all those memories wasn't something that I wanted to do right now.

"So what are you about to do?" Starr asked.

"I'm about to pack me a couple bags and get me a hotel. I know that Gio will be coming by and calling and I just don't want to deal with that shit right now," I replied.

"Well, let me go by the house and make sure that Amina is straight with Ma and I'll come up with some food and something to drink," Starr said.

"Let me call Caleb's sorry ass father and tell him that I need him to stay the night over there, and I'll be up also," Serenity stated.

I packed up my things, making sure that I grabbed a couple suits, my laptop and business phones and chargers. I put everything in the car and as I was doing that Gio called my phone.

"What, Gio?" I yelled into the speaker.

"I can't believe you did that to my car," he yelled.

"You fucking right I did. I'm sick of your shit," I replied.

"So you just going to end it like this?" he asked.

"Nigga, I have stuck by you when no one else would, and this is the thanks and payment I get? Another fucking baby and the bitch knew where I lay my head at."

I was so pissed that I was seeing red and shaking uncontrollably. He was saying something, but I couldn't focus on what he was saying, so I just hung the damn phone up. I blocked his number from calling and texting me. I have had enough of the lies and didn't want to hear anything out of his mouth.

Calling my cousin, I needed something to calm my nerves.

"Kash baby, what's up?" he asked.

"Aye, I'm coming through," I said.

"Oh word. How long?" he asked.

"I'm coming up in fifteen. You at the spot?" I asked.

"Yeah, pull up," he said.

WHEN I GOT to the area, he was sitting in his car with some chick on the passenger side. He hopped out the car and got in with me. He knew me like a book, so I had on my shades so that he couldn't see my eyes.

"What's up, cuz?" he asked.

"Nothing much. What's up with you?" I asked.

"Shid, business is lovely," he replied.

Sitting the weed in the cup holder, we sat there a little while longer and talked shit to each other. He got out of the car and walked back to the driver's side door. Once he got in, he looked at me with a face that I knew all too well.

"Tell that Gio he got to see me," I stated.

"What you talking about?" I replied.

"Kash, don't shit go on about you that I don't know about. Tell that fuck nigga when I see him, he got to get this work," he replied.

"Shyne, no. He isn't worth it."

"He ain't gotta be worth it, but it's a respect thing at this point. Aye, tell that baddie Starr that I'm on her trail," he said.

Pulling off, I headed to the nearest liquor store, grabbed us a couple bottles and a couple blunts. After that, I headed to the Marriott to get me a room for a couple days. Once I got to my suite, I unpacked my things, plugged my work phone and laptop up, and took me a shower. I texted Starr and Serenity the room number so that they didn't have to ask anyone and just come to the room. Walking out of the bathroom, there was a knock at the room, so I threw on my robe to open the door. When I looked through the peep-hole, it was Starr with what looked like a million bags in her hand.

"Hoe, open the door," she yelled.

Opening the door, I grabbed a couple of the bags out of her hand.

"What the hell is all of this, Starr?' I asked.

"I figured we all needed this break so I have a little of everything that we might need tonight," she replied.

I poured myself a drink, went to throw on some tights and a shirt and got on the couch. Starr walked out of the other bathroom in an adult onesie with a cup in her hand. By the time that Serenity walked into the room, we were two drinks ahead of her, and she had to play catch up.

"Y'all bitches started without me," she hissed.

"You were taking too long," Starr replied.

The whole night we sat up and talked about our dreams and aspirations and what we all wanted in a partner/husband. We were all single, and we agreed that we would start taking trips and going out like we were doing before.

When I woke up the next morning, I had a massive headache, and we were all laying in the California king bed with our clothes on. After calling room service to bring up some coffee and orange juice because I was thirsty as hell, I walked into the bathroom to relieve myself and brush my teeth. Coming out of the bathroom, I turned my work phone back on, and it started going off with a million notifications. Looking at some of the alerts, I instantly went over to the TV and turned on TMZ. They were showing video footage of my artist Smoove engaging in a fistfight with some other guy. Smoove was an R&B singer with a bad attitude that sometimes got the best of him. He is a great entertainer and performer- if he would get out of his own way and listen to people who care about him.

Between him and his worrisome baby mother, they were going to be the death of me. For some reason, she thought I was her personal assistant or something. I had to break it down to her more than once that I didn't work for her, but she just didn't get it. Picking up my phone, I saw that she had called me a million and one times and sent just as many texts.

Tara (Kyron BM): Please call me! I'm freaking out.

Tara (Kyron BM): Did you see the news?

Tara (Kyron BM): Why is your phone going to voicemail?

Tara (Kyron BM): I know you see these calls and texts.

SHE WAS RIGHT. I seen every call and text that she made, but my responsibility wasn't to her; it was about my client. She could wait for all I cared. I called my assistant Mico, and after instructing him to find out everything on what happened last night, I told him to come to my hotel room.

"Girl, where is the Aleve? My head is banging," Starr said.

"Look in the bathroom and bring me some too," I replied.

As Starr was walking to the bathroom, there was a knock on the room. It was room service with the coffee and orange juice. As I was pouring my cup of coffee, Serenity came out of the room looking crazy.

"Man, I haven't felt like this since that time we went to Vegas," she replied.

"Girl, we had a ball that week there though," I replied.

"Well, what you looking all stressed for?" Starr asked.

"My client Smoove got into a fight and got arrested last night," I replied.

No sooner than I finished my sentence, my phone rang, but this time it was my boss Barry calling me.

"Hello, Barry," I said.

"Kash, what in the hell happened last night? Why is Smoove's face plastered all over the place?" he asked.

"I have no idea, Barry. I haven't had a chance to speak with his manager," I replied.

"Get ahold of this situation, and I mean fast before it spirals out of control," he warned.

Hanging up from him, there was a knock at the door, and I went let Mico in.

"Y'all look like I was supposed to be here last night," he said, being extra as usual.

"Not now, Mico," I stated.

"Okay so I found out that he is in the county jail on a simple battery charge, but that isn't the real tea," he stated.

The next thing I know he was pulling out his phone showing me video of Smoove and the guy fighting with Tara's ass standing right there. Her ass was there the whole time and had the nerve to call and act innocent about everything.

"Fucking amazing!" I yelled.

Grabbing my phone, I called Smoove's manager to find out what happened and where was he.

"Yo!" Biz said.

"Biz, what the hell happened last night?' I asked.

"What you talking about Kash?"

"Oh my god, you mean to tell me you don't know what happened to Smoove? Where the hell are you?" I snapped.

"Nah, I bounced after his performance last night. They were going to the after-hours spot," he stated.

"I can't with you right now. I'll talk to you later." I hung up.

This the shit I'm talking about. This man is supposed to be

looking out for his client, and his ass is in bed and don't even know that the hell is going on.

"Girl, calm down. He got people," Starr said.

"It's not that easy, Starr," I replied.

I called the only person I could think of that could get his ass out of jail. My Father. He was the most in-demand attorney in the state of Florida and a beast in the courtroom. The phone didn't ring twice before he answered.

"Hey, Baby girl," he said.

"Daddy, I need a favor," I said.

"I was waiting on you to call," he replied.

"So you'll take his case and go get him out?' I asked.

"The only reason I'm doing this is because your name is linked to it. What's his name?" he responded.

"Kyron Sterling. Thank you, Daddy," I said.

"I'll text you when everything is straightened out," he said, hanging up.

2

Karter

"SO YOU'RE GOING TO THROW ALL THESE YEARS AND YOUR FAMILY AWAY?" Bailee yelled.

"Look, I'm not throwing my family away. I been telling your hard headed ass I was getting out of the game once I found the right person to take over for months. You just chose to ignore what I was saying and thought it was just a game," I replied.

What's up, I'm Karter Sterling. I'm 36 and the boss, but I decided to get out of the game or at least take a step back after I got knocked for having a couple kilos in my truck. One of my workers slipped up and put them in my truck instead of who they were intended for. Yeah, I know; a rookie move. Bailee is my soon to be ex-wife. Although I loved her to death, when I was locked down, she showed me a side of her that I didn't like. So I decided that once I got out, I would be divorcing her. She had become selfish and more concerned with money and the lifestyle that she was living.

When I got knocked off, I told her ass to lay low with the spending. What did her ass do though? Went out and bought a 2014 Range

Rover Velar fresh off the lot, paid in full. Now, what type of laying low was she doing? It felt like she was trying to bring more heat to me than the little charge that I did have. Bailee was the mother of my twin daughters and we were high school sweethearts- somewhat. I lived for her and the girls before I got locked up, but once I did, Bailee was out acting like she wasn't a married woman. I got reports from just about everyone that she was in the club, which I didn't mind because she was a grown woman and should know how to carry herself as such. The reports I got were of her flirting with niggas she knew I didn't fuck with and fighting in the club with her friends, just acting totally out of character.

When I would talk to her on the phone about what I had been hearing, she would cop an attitude and either hang up the phone or just give one the girls the phone. She acted like it was a major ordeal that she had to come and see me and bring the girls. Eventually, she stopped coming altogether and my father or mother would bring them to see me. She was acting like I was in jail for a long time, but I was only in there for three years.

"Look, I'm going to make sure that you and the girls are taken care of. I always told you that," I said, placing some clothes in a suitcase.

"What does that mean? I hope you don't think that you're going to leave me with these girls so you can find you a new bitch to spoil and live it up," she yelled.

"That's your fucking problem right there. You worried about what I'm going to do once I leave instead of trying to prevent me from leaving. You're selfish as fuck, and it's a shame that you don't even see it. My daughters will never be replaced; you, on the other hand, will," I replied.

Closing my suitcase, I headed down to my truck and threw my bags in. Then I went back in the house and into my office to grab all of my files and the important things that I had in the safe that she didn't know about. As I was walking about towards the door, she was coming down the stairs. She didn't even bother to say a word, and at this point, there wasn't anything that could be said to make me stay.

I had a connection at the Marriott, so I had called to let him know that I was coming. It took me about thirty minutes to get to the hotel, and the whole time that I was driving my pops was blowing my phone up. I figured that Bailee had called him telling him that I had left her ass. He finally texted me 911 when I saw that I knew it was something serious. I would call him once I got to my hotel room and got settled in. Getting out of my truck, I gave the valet my keys so that he could park and have my bags brought up to my room. My connect was working the front desk so all I had to do was give him the money, and he gave me the room key.

As I was unlocking the door to my room, there was room service and some dude waiting outside of the room across the hall. When the door flew open, there stood this chocolate goddess holding the door for everyone to come in. She was fussing so much about something that she didn't even notice that I was staring at her.

Putting my bags down in the bed, I sat down and called my pops back. While I was waiting for him to answer the phone, I turned on the TV and big as day, there was my baby brother's face plastered on the screen and not in a good way. Kyron had talent, but he also was a hothead with a bad temper. He was what some would call a wannabe thug. Don't get me wrong he was ready for anything, but that was something that he needed to change and badly.

"Nigga, I been calling you," my pops said.

"My bad, pops. I was dealing with Bailee and her dramatic ass. I just moved out," I replied.

"Yeah, well good for you. You finally seen the light. Your damn knucklehead ass brother done landed himself in jail," he said.

"I see. Let me make some calls and hit you back once I get some information," I replied.

"Yeah, let me know so I can get this pain in the ass of a girl from around here with all this damn crying and shit," Pops said.

"Who Tara?" I asked.

"Yes. Getting on all my damn nerves with this crying and asking questions and shit," he replied and hung up.

I had to laugh at pops because he was hell on Tara and Bailee. He couldn't stand their ass but dealt with them for the sake of our kids. If it didn't have anything to do with the kids, then he didn't want them around. He said that the vibe that they were giving off was bad. He always thought that Bailee was money-hungry, even when we were in school. But you know being in love and hard-headed, I had to prove him wrong. Looks like he was right after all in the end.

I called Biz, my brother's manager, to see what the fuck was going on. I pay him to make sure that my brother was straight, but from the looks of things, he isn't on the job. It wasn't like my brother was a child and needed to be watched; he just needed someone to watch his back while I was away.

"My dude, Karter. What's up?" Biz said.

"Nigga, this ain't no fucking social call. Tell me why the fuck my brother's face is plastered all over the TV and your ass in walking around freely and shit?" I questioned.

"When I left, he was heading to some after-hours spot with a few of his friends. He was in good hands, so I didn't think shit of it," he replied.

"Yeah, I see how good their hands were. Have you heard from him?"

"Nah, the only person that has called other than you was his PR person trying to find out what is going on," he stated.

"Well, I need to talk to dude so we can figure this shit out. Text me the nigga number so I can call them. I got to make a couple more moves."

"It's a female, and I got you," he replied, hanging up.

My brother was working all of my fucking nerves, and it wasn't even twelve yet. We talked about his expanding and doing a couple other things, but the way he was moving, his ass might not even be out to do the shit. While I waited for Biz to text me the number, I began to unpack my clothes and get comfortable. I was going to be staying here until I got my realtor to find me something nice to live in. He already had instructions to get with my pops and sell every house that I had except the one on the lake.

Although I was down for those little years, it didn't stop me from making money. Since I been out on paper, it looked as if I was the owner of a couple business with my father, but the truth was, I inherited the family business from my pops. We dealt with everything from guns to pills and business was lovely. While I was locked up, I informed my pops that it was time for me to fall back and let someone else take over for me. I still hadn't found that person that I wanted to put on so for the time being I handled everything still.

By the time that Biz texted me the number I was finished unpacking and was sitting on the balcony watching the kids at the pool. When my phone chimed, I immediately opened the text and dialed the number.

"Hello, this is Kashmir," the voice said.

"Yeah, I'm Kyron's brother Karter. Can you tell me what is going on?" I asked.

"Mr. Sterling, I'm in the process of getting him released now, my lawyer is already down there," she replied.

"Okay cool. I would like to meet with you so that we can discuss a couple of things," I said.

"That's fine but first, let me get Kyron situated and released, and we can link up for a meeting to discuss whatever you want to talk about," she replied.

She has a sexy ass voice, and I could only imagine what she looked like. She was all business and no play. I could tell that we would be getting along just fine. Straight and to the point just like I liked it.

I received a text from one of my daughters asking me if I had really moved out because petty ass Bailee had told her even after I told her ass I would explain to them what was going on. My daughters and I didn't have any secrets, so of course, I told her that I had moved out and that as soon as I was settled into my new spot, they would be coming over whenever they wanted. After I was able to calm her down, I told her to get ready for school and to call me when they got home for practice.

Me: You petty as fuck for that, B.

She always felt some kind of way 'bout my relationship with my daughters, and whenever she could get a chance to make me look bad to them, she did. I was on my way to Kyron's house when she decided to text me back.

Ex: Fuck you, I wanted them to know what a piece of shit you are

3

Kyron

I know Karter and Pops was going to kick my ass. They had been telling my ass to slow down before I crashed and here I was sitting in the fucking jail over some bullshit. It was all my baby momma Tara's fault. Her ass was in the club with another nigga, and when I asked where my son was, the nigga started rapping about that being his lady. I didn't give a flying fuck about that shit I just wanted to make sure that my shorty was straight. It was going on four in the morning and I knew damn well that KJ wasn't with my mom because she would've texted me like she always does when she had him.

While Tara and I were going back and forth, the nigga thought that it was a good ass idea to swing on me. I was a beast with my hands, so there was no need for anyone to help me. The next thing I knew the police was busting in the building and placing everyone under arrest. Now my ass is sitting here on this cold ass slab, mad as shit when I could've had my ass home.

"Sterling!" the Officer yelled.

"Right here!" I said.

"Roll out," he replied.

I was glad as shit to be leaving, but I hadn't had a chance to call anyone, so I was wondering who was getting me out. I swear to god if it was Tara bald-headed ass, I was fucking her up and walking the fuck right back in.

"There he is, Mason. I'll talk to you later," The officer said.

"Kyron Sterling? I'm Mason Pitts; I was sent by Kash, I'm your lawyer," he stated.

"I appreciate you coming," I said.

"No problem, whatever my daughter needs," he stated.

"Wait. Kash is your daughter?" I asked.

"That she is."

"I'll have to thank her when I talk to her."

HE OFFERED to give me a ride home and since there wasn't anyone waiting on me, I took him up on his offer. Getting into the money green Suburban with cream leather seats, I gave him the directions to my condo. Once I powered up my phone, it started going off with all the notifications and texts.

"We'll meet up tomorrow to discuss the case, I know you're tried so that can wait," Mr. Sterling said as I exited the truck.

The doorman opened the door, and I quickly jumped onto the awaiting elevator, pushing the button to the top floor. As soon as I opened the door to my condo, the smell of bacon hit me in the face. Walking down the hallway, I was met with a mug from my brother Karter.

"Damn, I thought I had slipped up, and one of my freaky bitches was here," I said.

"Man, cut the bullshit. What the fuck happened last night?" He asked.

"Tara thotting ass. I rolled up to the spot and her ass in there with her nigga or what have you, so I ask where KJ was. She started with the loud-talking, hand-clapping shit for attention and then her dude walked over. This nigga must've had something to prove and thought it was a great idea to swing on me. I rocked his ass. End of story," I stated.

"So, let me get this right, she around here calling pops like her ass so worried and she caused this?"

"Exactly, bro. The bitch sneaky, I been tryna tell y'all."

Karter finished cooking breakfast, and we made our plates and watched Sports Center in silence.

"So why the fuck wasn't Biz with you last night?" I questioned.

"Man, that nigga was trying to get his dick wet by some chick that he met at the club."

"I see. So tell me about this Kash chick?" he asked.

"I mean, she cool people, but she is definitely about her business and will curse my ass clear out and don't give a fuck."

"Oh word, she sounds like a beast."

"Man, a beast isn't the word. I'm waiting on her now to call and curse my ass out. I know her pops called her and told her that I was out."

"Her pops?" He asked.

"Yeah, her pops Mason Pitts," I replied.

"Nigga, he her peoples?"

As I was walking into the kitchen to put my plate in the sink, my phone rang.

"Speaking of her. What's up, Kash," I said.

"Nigga, don't what's up me. Why the fuck do I have to wake up and see your black ass on my TV?" She yelled.

"Kash, let me explain. It wasn't all my fucking fault, man."

"I don't give a fuck. I'm trying to clean up your fucking image and you fucking up everything that I'm working on."

"Man, come on, Kash. Where you at?" I asked.

"Pulling up to your building in five minutes and your ass better have on some fucking clothes," she said and hung up.

I couldn't do anything but shake my head while Karter was laughing at my ass.

"Man, she doesn't play with you at all," he said, laughing.

"Man, shut the fuck up, bro. You're going to love her and she easy on the eyes too."

"Good because I don't want to be working with no ugly bitch," he replied.

Before I could reply to him, the elevator dinged letting me know that Kash had arrived. I could hear her heels coming down the hallway and she was talking to someone on the phone.

"Yes, I'm here. I'll talk to you in a little bit, daddy," she said and hung up.

"Smoove, what I told you about being out there wildin' out and shit? You think these big ass companies want to endorse a hothead that can't control himself?

"Kash, I know and I'm sorry. I snapped when I saw my baby momma," I said.

"What the fuck are you talking about? Your baby momma?" she asked.

"Tara was there, she the reason I got locked up. I was fighting with her nigga."

"Oh, okay. She didn't tell me all that when she was blowing up my damn phone."

The whole time that she was talking I was watching my brother as he watched Kash move around the living room, snapping. Kash was wearing a skirt with her blazer and heels with her hair was pulled into a tight bun. She had now stepped out of her shoes and took off her blazer like she had done plenty of times before. Since I had been working with Kash, I consider her a friend, and we were comfortable enough to let our hair down and relax when needed.

"Kash, this is my brother Karter," I said.

"I'm sorry about that. Nice to meet you," she said, walking over to shake his hand.

"No need to apologize. It's nice to know that Kyron has someone else watching out for him other than myself," he said.

"I apologize about being so short with you earlier; my phone had been ringing nonstop," she replied.

"Spoken like a true businesswoman," he replied.

"Well, since we are here, what was it that you needed to speak to me about?" she asked.

As we all walked into the dining room, Biz came out of nowhere. Karter was sitting at the table just watching him.

"Biz, have a seat," Karter said.

I knew that Karter was pissed because I could see his eyes turn black, which meant he was about to snap or throw Biz off the patio.

"So, tell me again why the fuck your ass wasn't with my brother when I pay you and your so-called team to watch after him and have his back?" Karter asked.

"He is a grown ass man; it isn't my responsibility to watch his every move. What you want me to hold that nigga dick when he goes to piss?" Biz stated.

I saw a twitch in Karter's eye, and I know that shit was about to go all the way south. Karter pushed his chair from the table and went into the kitchen. I wasn't sure what was about to happen until the nigga came out with a frying pan.

Wamp!

"Nigga, I pay you to do what the fuck you gotta do to make sure he is safe!"

Wamp!

Karter was whipping Biz ass with the frying pan, and Kash was sitting there terrified. The shit was all new to her. If she was going to be dealing with me and my brother, she needed to get used to it because Karter ass would snap on the fly.

"I think I need to go," Kash said, standing up.

"Nah, you good, Kash. I'm about to wrap this shit up right now," Karter said.

"So, since you feel like making sure my brother is straight is too much for your ass, consider you and your whole crew off my fucking payroll. Get the fuck out of my face," he said.

As Biz got himself together, he walked to the elevator and got on but not before shooting a dagger at my brother. If he knows like I do, he would keep his feelings to himself because Karter or myself wouldn't hesitate to end his life.

"So Kash, say hello to Smoove's new manager. I got a couple of teams that I'm meeting within the next few days for security and shit," he said.

I had seen Karter like this before. When he in his 'I don't give a fuck' mood, anyone could get it. Whenever he was going through some major shit, he would lash out for the smallest shit, but this right here was something that I was going to have to get used to. It wasn't like we saw each other every day or even talked and now this nigga was going to be around 25/8.

"Well, now that you are the manager, I need to get all of your contact information so that all the upcoming events can be up sent to you. As soon as you get the security company secure, send me their info also so I can switch out the name and get them cleared," Kash rattled off, getting her bag.

Karter wrote down all his information, and Kash took a picture and sent it to her assistant. Within a matter of minutes, Karter's phone was going off with emails.

"We have the album release party coming up, so that means I need all that information back to me or my assistant before the end of the week," she stated.

As she got her things together, she told me to check in with her father and that she was working to get ahead of the bullshit and trying to get a statement prepared. No sooner than she was in the elevator, Karter was trying to get information on Kash.

"Aye, she got peoples?" he asked.

"That I don't know, bro," I said.

"Yeah, I can see now that she is going to be mine; it's all in her movement, bruh," he replied.

"Man, her ass ain't paying you no mind. She looks like one of those chicks that isn't into hood niggas just from the way she was looking when you knocked Biz upside his head," I said.

"With time, she is going to be mine. I just have to be patient."

"Yeah. Anyway, I'm about to take a shower, shit and smoke me a blunt. You know where everything is," I said, heading to my room.

"Bro, I'm divorcing Bailee," he said over his shoulder.

"What you say?" I stopped in my tracks.

"Yeah, I moved out and everything," he announced.

"Word? Well, that is good. It's been a long time coming. I can't stand her ass, but I love the fuck out of my nieces though."

"I just feel like a weight has been lifted off my shoulders. The whole time I was in prison, I couldn't focus because of the reports and shit that kept coming back to me. Like what nigga wants to hear that their wife was in the street turning up, fighting and shit like they weren't married? I'm not saying I wanted her to do the time with me but damn, at least be respectable about the shit," he said.

"Yeah, I feel you. The first thing that she wanted when you got knocked was the location of all the lockboxes and the codes to the safes. You know Pops shut that shit down with the quickness," I informed.

"Yeah, that's why I gotta get the fuck from around her before I kill her ass. I'm about to get up out of here, I got to make a couple more moves," he stated.

We dapped, and I made my way to my room so that I could shower. While the water was running, I sat down and rolled my blunt. I had been wanting one since I had gotten home, but everyone was here and shit. The water was nice and warm when I got in. I turned on the rain forest showerhead so it cascaded on my head. I had to get myself together. I had too much going on and way too much to lose to keep fucking up like some little ass boy.

Kashmir

I had to hurry and get from around Smoove's brother. His whole aura was doing something to me that I haven't felt in a while. He gave off a boss vibe and oozed with sexiness. From his walk to the certain way that he would talk had my panties dripping wet. As I was getting into my truck, Gio called me once again but this time from another number. I knew it was him because I had recognized the name.

"What, Gio?" I yelled into the phone.

"You ain't have to fuck a nigga shit up like that," he said.

"Priceless. Another bitch rolls up to my doorstep and tells me she had your baby and the only thing that could come out of your mouth is I didn't have to mess up your shit?"

"Kash, I love the hell out of you. I know I have a funny ass way of showing it, but I really do," he said.

"You can really kill all of that because I am cool on you and your lies," I replied.

"Can we talk about this?"

"There is nothing left to talk about, I have made up my mind that I am done. The door is closed on this relationship." Then I hung up.

I was now heading to the mall to find me something to wear tonight. I was about to let my hair down and shake this ass a lil' piece. I called Starr and Serenity on three way to see what they were up to and to see if they were coming out with me tonight.

"What's up, girl?"

"What happened?'

"Nothing has happened, ladies. I wanted to know if y'all wanted to step out tonight?" I asked.

"Girl, you know I stay ready to shake something," Starr said.

"I'm going; let me find a sitter."

"I'm headed to the mall now to find me something to wear," I said, pulling into the parking space.

"Aight. Well, I guess I'll go pull out something to wear to try to steal someone's man," Starr said.

"What time should we be at the hotel?" Serenity asked.

"I have a work meeting at five, so y'all come about ten. What club we going to?" I asked.

"Ooohhh, let's try Mirage. I heard it was nice as hell," Starr said.

"Okay then Mirage it is, ladies See you soon," I said and hopped out my car.

As soon as I entered the mall, Gio lying ass called me again.

"What, man?" I said.

"So you really changed the locks to the house?" he asked.

"Yes, I changed the locks to MY house because you are no longer welcome in MY house that I pay ALL the bills in," I replied.

"Baby, let's talk about this."

"I already told you that there is nothing to talk about," I said, hanging up.

THIS TIME I blocked his number, his mother's number and any number he ever called me from. I was now on a mission to find the tightest dress that I could find. I was in 'Fuck It' mode and nothing or no one could change that mood. I lucked out when I walked into BEBE and found a dress that I wanted to fit the mission. I purchased the dress and was off to my favorite boutique to find some shoes and accessories to match.

It was about three when I made it back to the hotel, and I was now starving, I headed over to the adjoining restaurant put in my reservation where I was informed there was about a fifteen-minute wait. I decided that I would head up to my room to drop off my bags, and when I returned, I could wait at the bar until my table was ready. When I returned back to the restaurant from dropping my bags off, my eyes landed on Mr. Karter himself sitting at the bar. I walked to the other side of the bar because he looked like he was deep in thought, and I didn't want to bother him.

When I took my seat, the waiter came over, and I ordered a Washington Apple.

"I see that you chose to ignore me a couple minutes ago, so I decided to come to you," a voice said behind me.

As I was about to respond, the hostess came over and informed me that my table was ready.

"Do you mind if I join you?" Karter asked.

"No, that is fine with me," I replied.

All the while, I wanted to scream hell no because the cologne that you are wearing has my panties ready to drop. Walking ahead of him, we were directed to our table where he pulled out the chair so that I could sit.

"So you know that you're too sexy to be dining alone, right?" he asked.

Bitch, he looks better than he did the last time that you saw him!

"Mr. Sterling, how may I help you?" I asked, trying to be professional.

"We are off the clock, please call me Karter," he replied.

"Since we are going to be working together, I think that we should share a meal and get to know each other," he replied.

"If I wasn't so hungry, I would put up a fight, but I'm not up for it," I stated.

"Well, that's a good thing because I could eat as well. So tell me about yourself."

"What do you want to know?" I asked.

The waitress came over to take our drink order, and I ordered a double Washington apple and he ordered Hennessey straight. He was licking his lips in the sexiest way I had ever seen.

"Everything. I want to know everything."

Good Lawd, why did he have to say it like that? He knew he was sexy and what turned women on with his cocky ass.

Get it together, Kash.

"Let's see. I grew up with my father and my bonus mother after my mother passed away from cancer, and I have a younger brother. My father is the top lawyer in the city, and I want to start my own PR firm in the next year or so,"

"A woman with goals, I feel you. What about a family of your own?"

"I would love to have a family. I just have to find a man that isn't a hoe out here in these streets," I replied.

"Maybe you're not looking at the right men."

"You may have a point," I agreed.

"So what is your vision for Kyron?' he asked.

"Kyron is very talented and has the ability to be one of the top R&B singers on the charts. This is if he could get out of his head and out his own way," I replied.

"I have told him the same thing a million times," he replied.

"I also believe that he needs to be around a completely different group of people. The ones that he is currently hanging out with do not have his best interest at hand. They are just around him to see what all they can get out of it; no one is really looking out for the brand,"

"I feel everything that you are saying, but how do we get him to break away from everything that he has been doing and the people that he grew up with?" He asked.

"I'm not sure, but that is where you would come in. You are not only his manager, but you are his brother, so I would think that you would know him better than anyone. From what I heard about you, before actually meeting you was that you were a force to be reckoned with," I replied.

"Ahhh, I see my reputation is still following me, huh?" he nodded.

As we sat at the table, we ate and exchanged ideas on how we could get Smoove to change his reputation. "I came up with the idea that every time he is in the news in a negative light, he would have to make a thousand dollar donation to the charity of our choice," I said.

"I like that, I like it a lot," he replied with a smile

OMG! His teeth are perfect.

With Karter liking the idea, I felt it would be the change that Smoove needed. I received a call from Mico letting me know that he was on his way over with the records that I had asked him to get from my father.

"I'm sorry I have to cut this meeting short. I have my assistant on the way with some information pertaining to your brother that I need to go over," I said, standing up.

"By all means do what you do best, I have the check," he replied, calling the waiter over.

While I was waiting on the elevator, Karter emerged from the restaurant and stood next to me. When the doors opened up, we both got on and went to press the same button. I was shocked because I thought a guy like him would have at least five houses that he lived out of. When the elevator got to the floor, he turned in the same direction that I was and headed down the hall.

"Are you following me?" I asked.

"Not at all, sweetheart. I'm heading to my room," he replied.

I stopped at my front door and low and behold, he was standing at the door across the hall, pulling his key out. Out of all the rooms in this big ass hotel, this fine ass man has to be sleeping across the hall from me.

As I was trying to get into my room, Mico with his extra self and Shannon came walking up.

"Well damn, this man in fione!" he yelled.

Shaking my head, I opened the door, pulling him inside and closed the door but not without taking a last look at Karter, who was staring at Mico like he had three heads. When our eyes connected, he winked at me, and I damn near lost it.

Taking off my heels, I got comfortable on the sofa, and we went to work. I had so many emails and things that I needed to get in order. We were about to go on tour, and I had to make sure that everything was together.

"So ma'am, you aren't going to tell me why in the hell we are in this hotel instead of your fly ass house by the pool?" Mico asked.

"Gio and I broke up," I replied.

"Thank God, I was getting sick of his trifling ass anyway," Mico replied.

As much as I wanted to be mad at him for his comment, I wasn't. It wasn't like Gio had the biggest fan club from my friends and family.

Karter

Kash was going to be my next wife, and she had no idea yet. No sooner than I closed my room door, Bailee was calling my damn phone.

"So you think that walking out is going to solve your problems?"

"There isn't any problems anymore because I'm out," I replied.

"What am I going to tell the girls?"

"Don't worry about talking to my daughters. I'll let them know the deal," I stated.

"I don't know why you think that you will find someone that will put up with your shit and treat you better than I did. Nigga, I helped you build what you have. Nobody is going to do half the shit I did," she yelled.

"You helped? The only thing that you helped me do is spending my fucking money. You weren't on none of the runs that I did or none of the dangerous shit I did for the family," I replied.

I was so tired of going back and forth with her ass that I just hung up the damn phone. I was over the shit with her and she was going to learn the hard way with me. As much as I wanted to choke the shit out of her, my mother will kill me if I put my hands on a woman.

Turning on the TV to Sports Center, I sat and watched Steven Anthony talk shit as usual. I poured myself a glass of Crown and started to relax. My mind began to wonder about this mysterious Kash; she has a certain fire and sass about her that turned me own. She was about her business and wouldn't hesitate to put someone in their place but in a nice-nasty way.

The ringing of my phone snapped me out of my thoughts of her. It was my best friend Ted; he and I been knowing each other since we were babies.

"What's up, man?' I asked

"Man, why your wife on the phone with my lady talking about you left her and the kids with nothing?' he asked.

"Come on, you know me better than that. True, I did move out of the house, but she still has money. I'm going to the bank and removing her off of my accounts and credit cards though. How I leave her with nothing when she has an account that she thinks I don't know about with about a hundred thousand in it?" I responded.

"I know, man. I just find it crazy that she would call us and start with the lies when she knows that we know you better than she does."

"I believe it. Look, I'm at downtown Marriott. I didn't feel like going to any of my other places. Come down, we need to chop it up a little about some things," I said.

TED WAS NOT ONLY best friend, but he was my accountant. When I got into the game, I made sure that both of us went off to college. I was smart with my shit, and I made sure that I had degrees, so when I did business, it looked official. Altogether I have about twenty different businesses that I didn't even handle, all that was up to my mom's. She was the face of our businesses. I know that this wasn't the life that my pops wanted for me, but who did he think was going to take over when he retired. Kyron damn sure wasn't prepared to do it, and I realized early.

We used some of our businesses to clean out money, mostly the strip clubs and no clubs because they brought in a lot of money in one night, so it was easy. That is where Ted came in. He made sure that everything that was going in was accounted for coming out. He also made sure that all our taxes were straight, so the Feds had no reason to come looking for anything. His wife Tanya was our attorney; she kept everyone nose clean.

My phone rang again, but this time it was my daughters. They were ten going on twenty.

"Hey, baby girl."

"Hey, daddy. Where are you?" she asked.

"I'm at a hotel; I moved out of the house."

MY DAUGHTERS and I had a bond like no other, I didn't sugarcoat shit when it came to them, and I kept things open so that they could talk to me about whatever. I hated parents that like to hide shit from their kids because they didn't want them to know things. Bailee was one of those parents, I guess she was brought up that way.

"I know Momma text me this long paragraph about it."

"Where are you?" I asked.

"I'm still at dance practice, and London is at basketball practice."

"Okay, what time does it end?" I questioned.

"We are done, I'm just waiting for mom to get here so we can leave."

"Ight, tell London to call me when she gets in the car. I'mma have your Nana come get y'all in the morning so we can have breakfast," I stated.

"Okay, Daddy. Love you," she said and hung up.

SOON AS SHE HUNG UP, Ted knocked on the door. Soon as I opened the door, he instantly started talking.

"Man, your wife is a piece of work. You know she still on the phone with Tanya," he said.

I CLOSED the door behind him, walked over to the living area and sat down,

"So what's up with baby boy, I see he ran into some issues?" he asked.

"He'll be fine. I'm taking over managing him, so maybe that will keep him out of trouble."

"That's the plan."

"So what is your plan because I know you're not staying here long?" he asked.

"Hell nah, I'm having pops sell off some of my properties."

"Smart move not putting them in her name, and having her ass sign a prenup," he said.

"I'm not trying to have her living in the gutter, but she will walk out of this marriage better than she walked into it."

"I feel you. Starting fresh."

"Exactly. The life that she and I lived was good, but it's more out there than watching over my shoulders hoping the Feds don't come at me again. She and I are on different paths, and I'm cool with that."

We sat and talked about some of the plans that I wanted to see happen with the clubs, and we decided that we would meet with the managers and go from there.

"You know she is going to make your life hell, right?" he asked.

"Well, she better be prepared then because if she goes quietly, it would be better for her. If not, then two can play that game and I always win,' I responded.

He stood up to leave, we dapped and he exited out of the door. I gathered my things so that I could go ahead and take a shower. As I lathered my cloth, my mind fell back on Kash, and my manhood became rock hard. Never had any woman had this effect on me that every free moment I found myself thinking about her. I had plenty of bad bitches in the past, but she was bad on another level.

Getting out of the shower, I wrapped my towel around my waist, and I laid across the bed. My phone chimed that I had received a text message.

Unknown: Have you talked to your brother?

Me: Who the hell is this?

Unknown: Kashmir.

Me: Oh no, I'll holla at him tomorrow. Don't you ever relax?

I changed her name in my phone.

Soon-to-be: I don't get paid to relax, especially working with your brother.

Me: We will have to work on that (Wink Emoji)

Soon-to-be: What does that mean?

Me: You will find out sooner than later, ma

I WAITED for her to respond, but she never did, so I turned the light off and watched TV until it ended up watching me.

KASHMIR

Once Mico and Shannon left for the evening, I began to get myself ready for the festivities. It had been a minute since I had been out with the girls. I had been trying to be the good girlfriend to Gio, but that shit blew up in my fucking face. I looked at the clock it was eight o'clock and I had told Starr and Serenity that we were leaving about ten, so that gave me just enough time to get myself together. I sat in the bathroom mirror and put large rods in my hair, since I was going to wear curls tonight. I began to take out my makeup so that I could give myself a soft beat. Then I turned on the shower so that it could warm up and turned on Pandora. As I step into the shower, I lathered up with my favorite Bath and Body Works scent, and my mind drifted to sexy ass Karter. I couldn't deny the tingling sensation that I was having in my kitty.

Jumping out of the shower, I ran to my suitcase and retrieved my bullet that I had tucked away; it was waterproof. I sipped on the drink that was on the bathroom counter and got back into the shower. My thoughts were on his lips. I imagined them all over my body and invading my kitty. I could tell that he worked out, and I wondered how long and thick he was and if I would be able to take all of him. With the bullet, it didn't take long for me to cream down my legs. Washing my body again, I wrapped my body in a towel and sat at the mirror.

I was now feeling good, I had my drink in my system, just gave myself an orgasm out of this world, and I was ready for tonight. As I was doing my makeup, I thought of the business plan that I was working on. I wanted to branch out on my own within the next six months from under my current employer. I was the best at what I did, and I currently had a list going of people who wanted my services.

There was a knock at the door snapping me out of my thoughts. I went to open, and it was Starr standing there, which was a surprise because she was never on time for anything.

"Damn bitch, you beat the hell out of your face," she yelled.

Laughing, I walked back to my room, slipped into my dress, and came back to the sitting room to wait for Serenity. Starr poured herself a drink as I scrolled through my phone. When Serenity finally arrived, I put on my shoes, and it was time for us to go.

"You're wearing the hell out of that dress," Serenity said as we waited for the elevator.

When the elevator finally opened up, imagine my surprise when I saw Karter with his sexy ass standing there in some basketball shorts and a tank top drenched in sweat. Taking the earbuds out of his ears, he stared at me like I was a piece of meat that he was ready to dive into.

"What's up, Kash," he said.

"Hey," I replied in a low tone.

"Damn, he is fine as hell," Starr said, causing him to laugh.

"You stepping out tonight?" he questioned.

"Yes, for a little while. Did you need me for something?" I asked.

"Nothing that can't wait until tomorrow. You enjoy your night," he responded.

We stepped onto the elevator, and as soon as the door closed, I was immediately questioned by both Starr and Serenity.

"That is my client, Smoove's brother Karter. Yes, I know he is fine. Believe me, it is hard to think straight around him," I said all in one breath.

"Girl, he staying on the same floor as you, I hope you throw some pussy out the door for him," Starr said, causing all of us to laugh.

Getting to the lobby, we walked out of the door and waited for the valet to bring my car around. It was going to take us a good twenty minutes to get to Mirage. Starr had turned on some Cardi B to get us in the twerking mood. By the time that we pulled up to the club, the line was wrapped around the building twice. I wanted to turn around and go back to the hotel.

"Now you know I'm not about to sit and wait in that long ass line," I said.

"Girl, come on. We won't even have to wait. The bouncer is sweet on me; I'll slip him my number, and he'll let us in," Starr said.

As we got to the front door, Starr whispered something in the bouncer's ear and stuck her number inside his pocket. Then he removed the velvet rope that let us in.

"See, girl, I told you that would work," Starr said.

We told the hostess when we walked in that we wanted a booth by the dance floor, so we didn't have to walk from the downstairs in order for us to dance. We ordered a bottle of Grey Goose and Patron along with pineapple and cranberry juice, as we watched the party-goers on the floor.

Once we sat down, the DJ played one of Smoove latest singles, it was a mixture between Chris Brown and Trey Songz and the club was eating it up. You had the guys that were standing around with their drinks in their hand, watching the ladies on the dance floor working as hard as possible to try to get their attention.

"Oh my God, this song is so lit," Serenity said as she sipped on her drink while dancing in her seat.

"Well, well, well. What do we have here, my cousin?" Shyne said.

"Hey, Shyne. What you doing here?"

"I just came to slide through real quick. What's good with y'all?" He asked, but the whole time he was staring at Starr.

"So are y'all hanging with us tonight or y'all going to be some hoes?" Starr asked.

"So, I see the cat didn't catch your tongue. Now, what's up, Starr? You not speaking tonight? But for real, we got a little section if you wanna come chill with us a little bit later," he replied.

I can see the disappointment in Starr's face when he said that. I don't know why she's playing hard to get with Shyne. He's a good dude, although he can be a hoe at times, but he still has a good heart.

"Oh, someone's in their feelings?" Serenity teased.

"You better quit playing around for you mess around and miss a good dude," I said.

As we danced with our drinks and laughed, Shyne kept the bottles coming, and we were feeling real good at the table by the time the night was over. Starr must have been feeling really good because she ended up making her way to the VIP section where Shyne was. She basically left us on our own while she had a good time with him. It was all good because she deserved to let loose, especially when it to come to Shyne.

"Yo, I'm not about to let y'all drive home like this," Shyne said.

"I'm ok; I can drive home," I replied, swaying from side to side.

"Bullshit. Unk is not about to kick my ass because I let you drive and end up getting a DUI," he replied.

Snatching my keys out my hand, he proceeded to walk to the front door, and we followed behind. It wasn't like we have much of a choice. Starr was getting in the front seat of my car while Serenity and I got in the back. He told a couple of his guys to follow us in his truck so that he could take Starr to Serenity's home once we got to my hotel.

"Yo, where you staying at?" he asked.

"I'm staying at the Marriott," I replied.

"Alright. The one downtown?" he asked.

"Of course, that's where I always stay."

"Oh, shoot. How are we going to get our cars home?" Serenity asked.

"I got a couple guys that can follow us. One can drive your car, the other one can drive my truck, and the other one can drive Starr's car so that everybody has a whip in the morning," Shyne replied.

Once we made it to the hotel, everyone jumped out of my car and Shyne jumped into his car with Starr while one of his homeboys drove Serenity home. I told him to let me know when they got home so that I can sleep well knowing they were in safe.

I had to stand back and watch my cousin giving out orders like he was somebody's boss or something.

"Yo Kash, you good to make it up by yourself or do I need to walk you up?" he asked.

"I'm ok. I can walk upstairs and get in my room."

"Alright. Well, let me know when you make it upstairs. Text me or something."

"Ok," I replied, heading into the entrance of the hotel.

Once I made it inside of my room, I text Shyne to let him know that I was inside, put my phone on the charger and got out in my bed fully clothed.

I was awakened out of my sleep by someone banging on my hotel door, and my phone ringing off the hook. I picked my phone up from the nightstand and Starr was calling my phone.

"Why are you blowing up my damn phone at this time of night?" I asked.

"So, tell me why your nigga came over here looking for you?" She replied.

As I walked to the door, I looked out the people, and it was no one other than Gio banging on my door.

"Bitch, you told that nigga where I was staying?" I asked in a whisper.

"Now you know me better than that. He didn't even get a chance to ask a question before I cussed his ass clean the fuck out."

"Well, how does he know where I'm staying?"

"Hell, I don't know. You always come to the same spot each and every time you have an argument," she replied.

The banging on my door continued for another two to three minutes, and then it stopped. When I went to open the door, Karter was there in his boxers, and a pair of Gucci slides. Damn. Even in the late morning, he looked good.

"You straight over there?" He asked.

"Yeah, I'm good. Sorry to wake you."

"You want to talk about this because if you got personal shit going on that's going to affect my brother, we need to clear it up ASAP," he replied.

"No, we don't need to talk about my personal life, and it won't affect the business that I'm currently doing with your brother. My personal life and my business are two different things, and I know how to separate the two," I snapped.

"Alright. Well, I'll get up with you in the morning then."

Once I closed the door, I went into the bathroom to shower since I was already up. As I was in the shower, I wonder what it would feel like to have Karter's lips to touch mine. They looked super soft and juicy. Stepping out of the shower, I dried off, lotioned my body up, and grabbed me something to sleep in. I was already up, so I decided to work a little bit on some of the contracts that we have for Smoove. I worked on that until I drifted off to sleep.

I woke up the next day refreshed with no hangover and ready to start my day. I was about to order some room service when I received a call from my brother Jaylin.

"What's up, baby bro? I asked.

"Nah, don't give me that. I saw ole boy in the club last night with some chick."

"Oh, that's good for him."

"Yeah, me and my niggas was going to roll up on him and beat his ass for the fuck shit that he tried but we to let him breathe. You good, sis?" he asked

"He probably was with his flavor of the night. Yeah, I'm good. I packed all his shit and took it to his bitch Kayla's house. She wanted him anyway so she can have him and his drama, along with the multiple baby mamas that he got."

"Oh word, it's like that? Had I known that I would've beat his ass off GP. It's about time you let that nigga go. He was wearing you down, sis. For real."

"Yeah, it was time. Plus I had Starr and Serenity with me," I said.

"If you had Starr with you, you was good anyway. There was no need for me to be there."

We talked a couple more minutes, and he told me that he would meet me later on for lunch. I haven't seen my brother in about a couple of weeks which was off for us. Because of his work schedule changing and me staying busy with Smoove, we kept missing each other. Once I hung up with him, I called room service and ordered me some coffee and something to eat. There was a knock at my door and I opened the doors to find Karter standing there looking good enough to eat.

"Good morning," his deep voice boomed.

"Good morning. Come in," I replied.

As he walked in the room, the scent of his cologne caused me to become weak. As he sat down, I realized that I was still wearing my pajamas that consisted of a pair of short shorts and a tank top with no bra.

"Give me one second to change."

Going into the bathroom, I brushed my teeth, washed my face, took off the bonnet that was on my head, and combed my hair out. I threw on a pair of pink tights and a tank top along with my slippers and went back into the sitting area.

When I returned, he was sitting down talking to someone on the phone.

"Nah, I want all of them houses sold but leave the one by the lake; that's my favorite one," he said.

I continued to listen to what he was saying.

"Yeah, Pops know to sign all the deeds to the houses. Make that shit quick, but I want a fair price for them shits."

"No worries, Mister Sterling. I got you, and I'll get the best price I can. I'll give you a call in a little bit," the voice on the other line said.

I cleared my throat so that he knew that I was in the room, and he looked at me, wrapping up his conversation.

"You know it's rude to eavesdrop," he stated.

"I wasn't," I lied.

"Shawty, I smelled yo' perfume before you even entered the room," he replied.

Thank god room service arrived when it did. I was starving, so when they entered, the first thing I did was grab a piece of bacon and poured me a cup of coffee.

"Have some?" I offered.

"N, I'm good. So, what was that about last night?"

"The guy that was at my door last night was my ex. He found me somehow, and he came up here. I changed the locks and blocked his number on my phone, so he had no way to contact me, "I replied.

"Well damn, what did that nigga do?"

"Acted like a dog face ass nigga and I'm over his shit," I stated.

"Miss Pitts, I didn't think you had it in you," he laughed.

"Had what?" I question.

"Some hood in you. I was beginning to think that you were stuck up and bougie."

"I'm far from them both on my off days."

"Well, it's refreshing to see a sexy woman about their business and can let their hair down when needed."

. . .

WHEN HE CALLED ME SEXY, my panties began to get wet like no other. He sat there watching me, waiting for me to respond to his comment.

"Well, I'm going to bounce I gotta make a couple moves," he said, standing up and walking to the door.

"I'll talk to you a little later."

Once we walked out of the door, I leaned against the door to gain my composure; this man knew he was fine. I can tell working around him was going to be a challenge for me because I already wanted to give him this snappa.

4

Karter

Yeah, shorty ass was feeling a nigga more than she wanted to. As I waited for the elevator, I texted my girls to see what they were up to, since I wanted to take them to breakfast.

Me: Hey, girls!
Paris: Hey, Daddy.
London: Hey.
Me: Y'all want to go get something to eat?
Paris: Yep.
London: Yes.
Me: 'Ight. Y'all get ready. I'm going to have Tank come get y'all.

TANK WAS the girl's driver, and he took them everywhere they needed to go since Bailee says that she was too busy to take them. After I texted him to go get the girls for me, I dialed my Pops number as I drove over to the restaurant.

"Damn, I'm glad a nigga wasn't dying or nothing." Was the first thing that he said.

"My bad, Pops. What's up?"

"You talked to your hard-headed ass brother?" he asked.

"Yeah, I went over there after he got out, I met with his PR person and fired Biz ass," I replied.

"Well good. Now what the rep had to say?" He asked.

"She cursed his ass clean the hell out, I just stood there and laughed at his ass."

"Oh, it's a woman?"

"Yeah and she bad too," I replied.

"Oh shit. I know what that means."

"Pops, I'm selling all of the houses and condos. I'm keeping the lake house, that is only one that she doesn't know about," I said, referring to Bailee.

"Ight. Well, let me know when I need to sign the paperwork, and I'm taking ten percent off the total amount," he replied.

"Damn, nigga. You taxing," I replied.

"You damn right," he stated.

"Ight man. Look, I'm about to meet the girls for breakfast, run some errands and will be over there later to see moms,"

"Give my grandbabies a kiss for me," he said.

I PULLED up to the restaurant and got us a booth. Once I was seated, I scrolled through the menu trying to decide on what I wanted to eat. Out of nowhere, a million texts came through my phone. As I was trying to read one, two more came in. Of course, they all were from Bailee talking reckless about how she going to find another nigga to be the kids' daddy and shit like that. One thing about me, I don't play games, and I wasn't about to play with her. I would slit her fucking throat, and I will raise my girls my damn self.

I didn't even feed into her bullshit because I know myself and I would send someone over to the house to fuck her up just because the shit she talking. The girls walked into the restaurant, and I could tell by their face that it wasn't good.

"Dad, you gotta do something about Mom," Paris said.

"What happened?" I asked.

"She is tripping about everything that we do now," London said.

"Y'all gotta be specific for me. Damn, I only been gone for one night."

"And that's how bad she been tripping since you left," Paris said.

"Okay, so last night when we got home from practice, we turned on our music like we always do to clean up and do our homework. Mom comes home about thirty minutes after we did, throwing stuff around after we just cleaned up and broke our Bluetooth speaker," London said.

"Ight, I'll talk to her," I replied.

We placed our orders, and I told the girls that I was selling all of the houses so if they had anything in any of them, they needed to let me know so that they could go and get it before then.

"Just make sure that we have enough room for us. The first thing mom said was that you were going to get you a new girlfriend and replace us," Paris said.

When she said that, I immediately became pissed, but I had to remain cool. What kind of mother would say some fucked up shit like that to her children? I couldn't take it any longer and had to send her dumb ass a text.

Me: One thing you will not do is try to turn my fucking kids against me. Keep our children out of this.

B: Fuck you, nigga

See, this is the type of shit I was dealing with. She wasn't mature enough to deal with this divorce like a grown ass woman. Instead, she wanted to act like a teenager and throw fits and shit, which I was over and could no longer take from her.

"So I am going to be working with your Uncle," I announced.

"Really? You working with Uncle Kyron?" Paris asked, excited.

"Yes, I'll be going on some of the tours and stuff. I'm just trying to get his business in order," I replied.

When I said that I was going out on tour, the first person that I thought of was Kash with her fine ass. Once the food arrived, we talked a little more before I paid the tab and walked the girls out to the car. Once the girls pulled off, I headed to my car to go see about Kyron.

I pulled up to his condo and took the elevator to his floor. When I walked in, he had a nigga walking around the place like he paid all the bills in this bitch and there was women sleep everywhere. It was almost like they partied last night, came back to his spot, and never went home. I went looking for him, only to find him in his room knocked the fuck out in the bed. I went to wake him, but he didn't budge. I had been telling him for so long to watch the people that he brings to his crib, and I see that he hasn't learned.

"Kyron, get the fuck up, man! You got a house full of people, and your ass is sleep," I yelled.

"What you talking about, bruh?" he asked.

"Get up, clear this fucking house and come holla at me on the patio," I demanded.

Walking through the people in the house, I made my way to the patio to smoke me a blunt. Kyron was stressing me the hell out already. After about ten minutes, the music stopped, and everyone was gone. Kyron walked out onto the patio with his own blunt and a lighter in his hands.

"What's so important that you had to come wake me up?" he questioned.

"You, nigga!" I yelled.

I could slowly feel the anger building up. I spent hundreds of thousands of dollars to make sure that he was able to live his dream, just for him to piss it away with the dumb shit.

"What I do?" he asked.

"Nigga, you out here wildin' out. First, you get arrested over some dumb shit with your trash ass baby momma- who I told you a while ago to leave alone. I come here to talk business, and you got niggas and bitches walking around this bitch like they own the shit and yo' ass in the bed sleep," I replied.

"We had a little kickback after the club last night."

"Kick that shit somewhere else. I told you about letting everyone know where you rest your head at," I replied.

"I know, bruh. I slipped up," he replied.

"WELL, we about to start moving completely different. All them niggas you got rolling with you, we changing that up. All them niggas ain't for you, they just along for the ride," I said.

"I hear you."

"Come on, have I ever led you wrong?" I asked.

"Nah, you be spitting some real shit to me."

"Well, my soon-to-be wants a total revamp."

"Who, nigga?" he laughed.

"You know I gotta have Kash. She fine as hell and I won't rest until she is mine,'

"Oh, you really feeling her, huh?" He asked.

"Yeah, she's a challenge, but I'm going to break her down," I replied.

"Yeah well, my money is on Kash," he laughed.

"We'll see. Look, let's step out tonight. It's been a minute, especially with me being a newly single man and all."

"Bet. You still staying at the hotel?"

"Yeah, I'm going to go hit Nick up to see if he can find me something temporary."

"Ight, I'm about to go shower then head over to see Pops. I know this nigga is going to curse me out when he see me," Kyron said.

"Oh yeah, he been waiting too. I'll come through once I make a couple more stops."

We dapped it up, and I left out to go handle the rest of my business. My first stop was to the bank. I was going to remove Bailee off of all of my accounts. She had took enough money from me, and I had been turning a blind eye, but the fact that she stole from me that was the icing on the cake. I wasn't a bad nigga, and I took care of her damn good. She didn't want for nothing, had a whole closet that still had tags on them, and she still brought more. Somewhere along the lines, she turned into this materialistic chick that had to flaunt what she had, instead of playing it cool.

While I was waiting on the branch manager, I sent Nick a text to see if he would be in the office. I wanted to talk to him about a couple things. He said that he wouldn't be there until later on this evening so I could stop by when I got a chance. Nick was my dude since high school, he was a cool white boy, but you could tell that he had a little hood in him. His family moved to my neighborhood the summer before high school. His parents were just like mines except they were white, but you couldn't tell Nick's family that they weren't black. They were at all the cookouts, spades games and talked more shit than a little.

"Mr. Sterling, I'm Tiffany Hayes, the branch manager. Follow me," the woman said.

We walked into her office and sat down. She was a light skinned chick with a tight bun in her head. She was wearing a suit that fit her well, and her ass was fat as shit.

"So how can I help you today?" She asked.

"I would like to remove the authorized signer off my account," I replied.

"Okay, I can help you with that. May I see your driver's license?" she asked.

Placing my license on her desk, she was a cute chick, but she wasn't my type. She was the type that put up a good front but didn't know the first thing about taking the pipe once it has been laid down.

"To remove the signer off the account, we can do it two ways. We can start a new account with just you on it, or the signer can sign a release removing themselves off the account," she stated.

"Let's just open new accounts, it's easier that way," I replied.

After spending about an hour in the back, I finally had all the accounts straightened out. I knew that I would hear from Bailee once she tried to use her debit card. I canceled her credit card that she had also. She was going to be pissed, but right now I didn't even care. I wasn't completely heartless, so I left twenty grand in the account if she wanted to come and get it out. I had all my ducks in a row with the lawyers, so I was ready for a fight. If she knew like I knew though, she would take what I was offering and move the hell on.

I pulled up to Nick's office and locked my car. I knew business was doing well because the lot was almost full. I had been talking to him about expanding since he had outgrown his current space.

"Hey, Karter. He's in the office," Shanna, Nick's wife, said.

Walking into the office, Nick was talking on the speaker to someone. As I was walking around the office, I noticed that he had one of my houses up on a board. Nick was a beast in the real estate game, and everyone came to him for the best, and he always got top dollar.

"What's up, man?" Nick said.

"I need to get me a lil' spot ASAP, this hotel living isn't for me," I replied.

"What you have in mind?" he asked.

"I could do a condo or something, for now, but make sure that it has enough room for the girls," I stated.

"Of course, it will have space for my nieces. Question. For the houses, are you selling those furnished?"

"It doesn't matter to me. If Shanna see some stuff that she wants to get, she can have it. Especially for staging the house and stuff for the open house. You get any bites on the houses? I know we just put them on the market," I asked.

"Actually, I'm showing three of them tonight. One of my friends has a couple people new to the city, and they loved your house when they drove by it," Nick said.

"Well, let me know what you come up with for me, and then we will go to work looking for a permanent home."

"Ight man. I'll let you know what I got."

"Good shit. I'll holla at you later," I said, walking out of the office.

"I heard you and Bailee are finally done," Shanna said.

"Yeah, sis. It's time to let it go," I replied.

"Well, good for you. Let me know if you want me to hook you up," she laughed.

"Nah, I got my eye on someone already," I replied.

5

Kyron

I was heading to my parents' house to hear my Pops' mouth about how I was fucking up. I was trying to prepare myself because Pops went har. I knew the first thing he was going to go in on was Tara. He and Karter weren't her biggest fans; they always felt that she was with me for the clout. I was so blind to the things that she was doing. I didn't even notice until we broke up and I started to see a side of her that I didn't like. As I was driving, I received a call from her. She had been blowing my phone down since yesterday when I turned it back on.

"What the fuck you blowing up my line for, man?" I asked.

"I was calling to see if you were safe and okay," she replied.

"Yeah, I'm straight. No thanks to you. Look don't hit my line unless it is about my son, we ain't together, so there isn't anything else to talk about," I replied.

"What you mean, don't hit your line?" she questioned.

"You heard what I said. If you need something, hit up Nisha and she will get you what you need."

"I'm not going through no one to speak with you. You done let this little fame go to your head," she yelled.

"Nawl, that's not it, but I can't deal with all the drama coming from you. So if you want me to get my son or need something, hit up Nisha. Or better yet, hit Dukes up; she'll take care of you," I replied and disconnected the call.

I needed to stop and get me a blunt to relax myself from Tara dumb ass. As I was getting out of the truck, I caught the tail end of this chick ass. Baby girl was stacked. I did a quick jog into the store to see if I could get another quick glimpse. I walked to the coolers to grab me something to drink when I came face to face with this chocolate beauty. She stood about five foot six with thick thighs and hips to match. She had her hair in a bob and kind of reminded me of Juju for Love and Hip Hop, but she was Puerto Rican. Walking up to the counter, I put my stuff down.

"Aye, add her total to mine, my dude," I said to the clerk.

"You didn't have to do that," she replied.

"I know," I replied and walked out of the store.

"Hey, thank you," she called behind me.

We both made our ways to our cars when I noticed that she was about to pump her gas. Being the nigga that I was, I wasn't about to let her pump in my presence.

"So, pretty lady, do you have a name," I questioned.

"Yes, it's Serenity." She blushed.

"Nice to meet you. I'm Kyron."

"I know exactly who you are," she replied.

"If you know who I am, why don't you let me get them numbers, and we can do dinner or something?"

She went into her car to retrieve a pen and a piece of paper.

"Ma, just put the number in my jack, and I'm going to call you right here to make sure that you didn't give me the wrong number," I stated.

"Nah, I don't play them type of games,' she replied.

WE CHOPPED it up while I finished pumping her gas and I told her that I would hit her up later once I finished taking care of some business. Shorty was wearing the hell out of them shorts that she had on. She paired them with some J's and a t-shirt, but I could tell that she knew how to really turn on the sexy when needed.

I pulled up to my parents' house and put the code in to unlock the gate. Everyone had their own code, so there was no way for it to be hacked. My pops was big on the protection of my mom's. He was in the game before he gave it over to Karter, so he knew how niggas got down. When there was beef, the first thing they wanted to do was hit a nigga family and Pops wasn't having it at all. My pops did well for himself without getting caught. He had sense enough to get his money, pass the business on, and get out.

He had been making moves behind the scene in Karter's absence. I had been assisting when I was needed, but neither one of them wanted me getting my hands dirty too much.

"'Bout time you brought you ass over here, nigga," Pops said as soon as I walked in.

"Yeah, I came over here to finally get my curse out over with and see my main lady," I replied.

"Yeah, well take your ass on in there. She been fussing since yesterday when you got out," Pops said.

I walked into the sitting room where my mom was watching that nigga Steve Harvey; she loved that show. The moment that she saw me walk through the door, she turned down the volume and just stared at me.

"Ma, you don't have to say it, I know that I got to do better. I'm done acting like an ass over dumb shit especially behind Tara's ass," I stated.

"Watch your damn mouth, boy," my pops said, sitting down.

"Kyron, you have so much potential, but that attitude of yours isn't going to get you far. Those people you hang around don't give a damn about you, and they ain't shit either. I can feel that in my spirit," she said.

"I know. Karter is taking over as my manager so things will surely be changing," I replied.

"Well good. He'll get you and your raggedy ass friends together."

As we were talking, Karter walked in.

"What y'all in here talking about?" he asked.

"We in here talking about your hard-headed ass brother," my mom replied.

"Oh yeah, he going to be straight now. I got him," Karter assured.

"So you finally did it, huh?" Mom asked.

"DID what?" Karter replied.

"Left Bailee ungrateful ass," she said.

"Ma, what's with all this cursing? I'm not used to this at all," I said.

"Boy, shut the fuck up. This side has always been there; I just didn't show it a lot."

I HAD to laugh because hearing her curse caught me off guard, and I was going to have to get used to it. She always talks so sweet and kind that I believe that my mother was as pure as they came with a heart of gold.

"So what are we going to do about my grandson?" Pops asked.

"Well, I have cut off all communication with Tara, and I instructed her to call Nisha or Ma- if that is alright with you," I said to my mother.

"I guess I can hold my tongue long enough not to beat her ass," she replied.

"Well, play nice for the sake of KJ," I said.

"I will but if she steps out of line, just know that I won't hesitate to call Shakey and Dovey to wear her ass out," she said.

My mom had my side hurting because she was so serious about getting my cousins on Tara.

"Ight, I'm about to bounce. I gotta make a couple moves before I hit the studio tonight."

I had plans on hitting up shorty to see if she wanted to meet up later on. I wanted to go to my crib and get things in order since it was a mess and the maid wasn't coming until Thursday.

.   .   .

"OK KYRON, BE GOOD," mom said.

As I walked out of the sitting area, Karter followed behind me.

"Aye, you heard from shorty?" He asked.

"Not today. Why you ask?"

"She had some nigga banging at her hotel room door last night. I started to knock his ass out with all that fucking noise he was making," Karter informed.

"Wait, how do you know that?' I questioned.

"I have the suite across the hall from her. Get your mind out of the gutter," he replied.

"Well, it probably was the nigga that she beefs with all the time. From what I hear, he is a real fuck up," I stated.

"Ight. I'll hit her up later on. I want to go by the house and grab a couple things while Bailee is at the store," he said, walking to his car.

6

Kashmir

After Karter left, I finished my breakfast and decided to go down to the gym for a quick workout before I headed into the office. I hadn't planned on going into the office today but with the recent drama with Kyron's ass, I figured that I would show my face, so all the whispering and finger-pointing could take place.

I got onto the treadmill, put my cordless Bluetooth on Kevin Gates and did five miles. Running always made me feel better when I was stressed, and the drama with Gio and Smoove had my head spinning.

Once I finished my run, I felt refreshed and ready to start my day. I went back to my room, showered, and headed out to the office. As I was walking into the building, Mico called me.

"Yes, Mico?"

"Hey, boss lady. Mr. Green would like to have a meeting with you," he replied.

"Well, it's a good thing that I am walking into the office now, huh?"

"I'll see you in a sec," he replied.

As I was getting off the elevator, Mico was standing at his desk with my coffee and the file that I needed for Smoove. I walked past him and headed into my office to set my things down. I knew this meeting was about Smoove; I could feel it. It was bad enough that Mr. Greene didn't want to take Smoove on as a client, but now his face is plastered over TMZ and other gossip blogs.

"Call Kristin and let her know that I'm ready if Mr. Greene is ready," I said to Mico.

Mico walked back into my office to let me know Mr. Greene said he was ready when I was. I grabbed both of my phones, put my blazer on, and headed over to his office. I knocked on the door, waiting for him to signal for me to come in.

"Mr. Greene, you wanted to see me?" I asked.

"Yes, come in and close the door," he replied.

Before I could take my seat, he was already asking me a million and one questions.

"So, what the hell is going on with Smoove? How is it that he ended up arrested and on TMZ?

"He got into a fight with some guy that his child's mother was with. Words were exchanged, and fists were thrown. He was arrested and released with a lawyer that I retained," I replied.

"Who is his manager?" he asked.

"Well, his new manager is Karter Sterling, who is Smoove's older brother. He will be taking over everything and revamping everything," I replied.

"How do you think that this will work out?" he asked.

"He is 99% better than the previous manager and is business-oriented so this should be a good move."

As we were talking about different strategies for Smoove, Mico interrupted our meeting after informing me that I had a visitor. When I walked into my office, there stood Gio with roses and a teddy bear.

"What the hell are you doing here?" I asked as low as I could.

"I came to talk to you," he replied.

Walking to my desk, I picked up my office phone calling the security desk. I didn't have time for this shit and the fact that he thought that he could come with these tired ass flowers and a bear he probably got from Walmart, really pissed me off.

"Yes, can you come to my office, please?" I asked and hung up the phone.

"Look, I know I fucked up but just give me a chance to explain," he stated.

I sat there staring at him. I didn't have anything to say to him. There was a knock at the door and security walked in.

"So you really called security on me when I came to talk to you like an adult."

"You can walk him out," I said to security.

"This is foul as fuck," he said.

Closing the door to my office, I plugged in my phone, so it could charge and got to work. Although I was the Director of PR, I still had others that I needed to take care of business. I couldn't let my personal life interfere with my business. The only reason I was working with Smoove was because I was the best, and I was requested by his label. Mr. Greene had this cookie-cutter type of employees and entertainers that he wanted to be surrounded with. He definitely didn't have a lot of R&B or Hip-Hop artists. It was that exact type of stuff that made me want to branch out on my own.

We could have fifteen people apply for an opening, and they wouldn't get hired because they weren't experienced enough or didn't meet the standard. I probably would've hired a good number of then because they could be trained if they were willing to learn. I received a text from Karter that I wasn't expecting.

Karter: I think we need to get an all hands on deck meeting ASAP!

Me: Sounds like a plan. Let me know when and where.

Karter: Cool. I'll hit you up later.

I FINISHED WORKING on the files and left out of the office, telling Mico that I was gone for the day and that if he needed me to contact me on my cell. I was about to head over to my father's house when my security company called me informing me that my alarm was triggered and wanted to make sure that I was okay. I told them that I wasn't home and hadn't been for a couple of days and to please send the police.

I pulled out of the parking lot like a bat out of hell, heading to my house. When I arrived, there had to be about ten police cars at the house. I jumped out of my car with it still running and went to the first police officer that I could find.

"What happened?" I asked.

"Ma'am, are you the owner of this resident?" he asked.

"Yes."

As I was standing there waiting for my house to be cleared, one of the nosy ass neighbors walked over to me and informed me that it was Gio that threw bricks through my front window and doors. In my eyes, that was a total bitch move, and now I was going to let my cousin Shyne whip his ass. I was pissed as hell, so I called my brother and Shyne so that they could have someone come fix my door and my window.

Gio thought that I didn't know that he worked for Shyne, but Starr let it slip one night when we were hanging out. I talked to Shyne, and he only messed with him because of me, he can kiss that shit goodbye.

Me: I can't believe that you brought your broke ass to my house and threw bricks through my windows and doors. That is a fuckboy move.

Liar: I bet that got your attention though.

As I was about to respond, Shyne called me. He didn't even give me the time to say hello before he started talking.

"That nigga gotta see me and that's on moms."

I knew Shyne was pissed because he never put anything on my late aunt unless he meant it.

"I know, cuz," I replied.

"My niggas on their way to look at the windows and door. We trying to get the glass company to come out tonight to check them out also."

As soon as I hung up from him, Karter called me.

"Hello."

"Kash, you straight?" he asked.

"No. My fucking dumb ass ex threw bricks through my windows and door, and there is glass everywhere."

"Kash, calm down. Send me your location," he replied.

"Karter, I'm okay. You don't have to worry about it."

"Kash, did I ask you all that? Send me your location now," he said and hung up.

I sat there looking at my phone dumbfounded until a message came through

Karter: Never mind. I'll be there in ten minutes

Who in the entire hell did he think he was, bossing me around like I'm a damn kid or something? I was starting to clean the glass up when Karter, Shyne, and my brother all walked in, smiling and laughing and shit like they were friends.

"Kash, you didn't tell me that you knew this dude," Shyne said.

"You know him too?" I asked.

Damn, Karter was standing there looking all godly in his all-white Gucci shirt and pants with his Gucci loafers. It was the total opposite from what I had seen him in before.

"Shyne and I do a little business together," he replied, staring at me like he was looking into my soul.

"Kash, what you got to eat in this bitch and where is the beer?" my brother asked.

"How about you take your ass in the kitchen and see?" I replied, heading upstairs to my room.

I needed to change out of my clothes to finish getting the glass up. I was still walking around in my work clothes and shoes. As I was changing, I could hear someone on my patio downstairs. I peeked over the railing to see that Karter was talking to someone on the speaker.

"So you just going to close the bank account out so that I wouldn't use it without any warning?' the voice said.

"You damn right. I pulled all of my money out of the account you got over a hundred and fifty grand sitting in an account that you thought I didn't know about. Look, I'm trying to be fair about this. You can have your cars and the house. All of my cars will be coming with me, but you won't steal from me. That is the quick way to die and you know that. Had you stopped to see what was in the account I left, you more than enough to take care of the household bills for a good lil' minute."

I stood there thinking to myself, what kind of fuck up was she to lose out on a sexy ass man like Karter. As they were wrapping up the call, I slid back into my room to finish getting dress so that I could head back downstairs. By the time that I made it downstairs, Karter was walking into the living room. I walked into the kitchen to get me something to drink to ease my nerves. I don't know why, but when I'm around him, my nerves are on high alert.

"Yo, it is rude to eavesdrop, Shawty," he whispered in my ear.

Lawd, I could've melted into his arms when he whispered in my ear. I turned around to say something to him but was caught off guard when he pressed his lips against mine. I welcomed in his tongue. It felt like time had stood still; that was how intense the kiss was. When we finally broke away from each other, I had to stand still for a minute to gain my composure.

"Damn, I been wanting to do that since I met you the other day," he said.

I didn't know what to say. I just stood there like an airhead shaking my head up and down.

"Kash, man, a nigga hungry; order some food or something," Shyne said, walking in the kitchen.

"Okay. What do y'all want?" I asked.

"We will finish the conversation, later on. Order the food and use this card," he stated, handing me his AMEX black card.

7

Karter

I couldn't resist kissing Kash; it was something that I had been wanting to do since yesterday. Her lips were soft and juicy. If it wasn't for the fact that her brother and cousin was there, I probably would've tried to take it a step further. While we waited for the window company to come board up the windows and door, I would steal glances at Kash to find her looking at me, blushing. I told Shyne to put some men at her house so no one would try to come in. While I was sitting there shooting the shit with them, my pops called me.

"What's up, old man?"

"You tell that soon to be ex-wife of yours do not call here upsetting your mother with her bullshit," my pops said.

"What are you talking about?"

"Bailee called here talking about how you closed out all the accounts, how she and the kids don't have any money to live off of and talking about you was going to pay for that. Well, your mother being who she is, went the hell off. I had to stop her from going over to the house," my pops laughed.

"I got her, Pop. For now on, don't answer any calls from her either," I said.

Hanging up from him, I announced that I had to make a couple moves but would be back to follow Kash to the hotel. I ran out of the house with one mission, and that was to choke the shit out of Bailee for trying my ole girl. She knew better than to play with me, but my ole girl was another story. It took me about twenty minutes to get to the house. When I arrived, there were cars in the driveway, which wasn't anything new, Bailee always had someone at the house.

When I walked into the house, there was music playing, and I could hear talking from the back of the house. I walked to the back, and her ass was having a pool party of something with all her lil' friends.

"Well, isn't it the man of the house," her friend Tashia said.

Not even bothering to speak, I went over to Bailee cause I wanted to talk to her alone,

"Can I rap with you for a minute?' I asked.

She already knew by the look on my face to get up and walk off so we could talk in private. As soon as we closed the patio door, I wrapped my hands around her throat.

"Don't you ever call my mom's talking reckless again. I will break your fucking neck with my bare hands," I said to her.

Her eyes began to fill up with tears, but I wasn't falling for it, all the love that I had for her was gone. I tried to make it work once I got out, but it was no use. I left her in the kitchen gasping for air, went into our bedroom and removed the rest of my clothes. Then I went into my man cave and removed everything out of the safe that I had there. Bailee never came into my cave, so she didn't know about that safe that I had.

When I walked back into the kitchen, she was sitting at the dining room table looking at her phone.

"The movers will be over tomorrow to move the rest of my stuff and the cars. Please don't give them a hard time," I said and walked away.

I wanted to go to the lake house to drop off the stuff that I had in my car but decided that I would go tomorrow and headed back to Kash's house. When I arrived, Shyne and Jaylin were gone, and the window company was there taking measurements for the windows and door.

Kash was now sitting at her dining room table with her laptop open and a glass of wine. I noticed that she was wearing glasses and looked even sexier than before.

"Shyne and my brother said to call them when you got back," she said.

"Damn, them the niggas ate and bounced?" I replied.

"I made you a plate, it's in the microwave," she stated.

ITS'S BEEN a minute since Bailee fixed me a plate, let alone put one up for me. The only person that would ever do it was moms. Being a wife and mother certainly wasn't Bailee's strong suit. She liked the title but didn't like the responsibility that came with it.

"When the guys finish with boarding up the place, you want to head back to the hotel?" I asked.

"You think that I should leave with my house like this? No, sir. I'll stay here tonight," he replied.

"Well, if you're staying, then I'm staying also."

"Karter, you don't have to do that."

"I know. I don't have anything else to do anyway."

"I do need to go to the hotel to grab a couple things though,' she said.

"Well, let's ride. I have someone sitting on the house, so it will be okay while we are gone."

She went upstairs to change her clothes and came back down with her hair out of the bun that it was in. We made it to my car, and she reached for the handle. I smacked her hand.

"What the hell was that for?' she asked.

"Never reach for a handle when you are in the presence of a man, Shawty," he replied.

"Well, go head and open the door then," she blushed.

She eased into my car, I got into the driver's side, and we rode out. I kept looking at her as she texted on her phone. Whatever she was talking about had her smiling from ear to ear. We pulled up to the hotel, and I pulled out a couple things that I wanted to take inside.

"I'll be about ten minutes," Kash said.

"Take your time, Shawty. I'mma pack me a bag," I replied.

Being as though we were out this way, I was planning on going to the house at the lake, which was about an hour away to drop off the rest of the stuff in my car. There was a knock at my door, I looked through the peephole, and it was Kash standing there. I opened the door and invited her in so I could finish getting ready.

"I need to make a quick run to drop some stuff off. You don't mind riding with me, do you?" I asked.

"No, it's fine. I could use a little getaway for a while," she said.

I grabbed my bag, and we walked out of the room. I handed the valet my keys when I heard my name being called. I turned around, and it was Bailee ass standing there. The first thing I wanted to know is how in the hell did she find me.

"Go ahead and get in the car," I said to Kash.

"Is this the reason you are leaving your family? For that bitch?" she yelled.

"B, get the fuck out of here with the dramatic ass shit. You know exactly why I'm leaving you. Not my girls, but you," I said.

She walked over the Kash's window and knocked on it. I was shocked when Kash rolled it down.

"May I help you?" she asked.

"Yeah, you screwing my husband?" Bailee asked.

"Sweetie, if I was screwing your husband, you would definitely know it because this right here would not be going on," she replied and rolled her window back up.

I stood there with a smirk on my face because Kash handled Bailee with class and poise. I walked around to the driver's side, got in, and we headed out to my lake house. I made sure that Bailee crazy ass wasn't following me, but her ass was blowing up my phone so bad that I turned it off.

"So, what was all that about?" she asked.

"I'm divorcing my wife. After I got out, I looked at her differently. I was so busy being the Kingpin that I didn't notice what everyone was telling me."

"I see."

"I like how you handled that though, Shawty."

"Look, I have enough drama going on that I don't need to argue with a woman about her husband. I mean, you sexy as hell but I ain't that chick," she replied.

"What chick is that?" I asked.

"The type to willingly sleep with a married man."

"Even if the man is separated?" I asked.

"If it's a legal separation, then I would have to think about it," she replied.

"So if I was legally separated, I would have a chance?"

"How did we get on this subject?" she asked blushing.

"You opened the door."

"I would have to think about it. I mean, you are my client's manager, I wouldn't want to mix business with pleasure."

"Oh, I have no problem with the mixing of the two. The question is, could you handle it?"

I noticed that she started to squirm in her seat; she was turned on and didn't want to admit it. Little did she know, I was going to wear her down, little by little.

8

Kyron

I WAS SITTING in the studio playing back a song that I had just finished when my security Duke walked in with Serenity fine ass. Pausing the music, I stood up to give her a light hug. Shorty was bad as fuck. I could tell that she had on light makeup with a maxi dress and some Tory Burch sandals with some pretty ass toes that look freshly painted. She kept it simple and cute, and I was digging the fuck out of her look.

"That song sound fiyah," she said.

"Thank you, sweetie. So what do you want to do?' I asked.

"Whatever you would like to do," she replied.

"How about I finish with the song and then we can go and get something to eat?" I said.

"Sounds like a plan to me."

I turned on the song that I was working on, I still had a couple of tracks that I needed to lay down, and I had to finish it tonight in order for it to be ready for my album release party in a couple of weeks. I was in the booth while Serenity was watching me do what I did. It took me about an hour and a half to get the song the way that I wanted. I was a perfectionist, so I couldn't help it.

Once we were finished, I grabbed my phone, Serenity got her purse, and we jumped into my whip and headed to my favorite restaurant for dinner. When we pulled up to Ruth Chris, I told the hostess we needed a table, and we were seated almost immediately. We looked over the menu, but I already knew what I wanted, so I was just waiting on Serenity.

"So tell me about yourself?" I said.

"Well, I'm 28, I'm a social worker and I have one son that is five years old. He is currently at my best friend Starr's house with my goddaughter. I don't deal with my son's father because he is an asshole and I like Chic-fil-a," she said.

"Wait, how you end it with I like Chick-fila?" I laughed.

"I thought that I would lighten the mood," she laughed.

As we were talking the waitress came over, and it was the last person that I wanted to see.

"Hey, I'm Nina. I'll be your server for tonight. Hey, Kyron," Nina said.

"What's up, Nina?"

"Is this the new flavor of the week?" she asked with a smirk.

"Look, are you going to take our order, or do I need to get your manager to get a new waitress? You know what? Don't answer that. Aye, Ronnie!" I yelled.

The manager of the restaurant walked over to us, and I pulled him to the side so that no one could hear what I was saying.

"My dude, me and Nina have a past. I'm here on a little date you see, and I don't want her to mess it up. She is kind of spiteful so please give me a new waitress and make sure she is nowhere near our food," I said.

"I see, Mr. Sterling," Ronnie said.

We walked back to our table, and I sat down as he whispered something in Nina's ear. She rolled her eyes and walked away.

"What was that about?" Serenity asked.

"I used to mess with her a while back on and off, but I cut things off with her once my son was born because she was messy as hell," I replied.

"Oh ok. So am I the flavor of the week?"

'Nah, sweetheart. If you were the flavor of the week, we damn sure wouldn't be sitting down to eat nowhere. I would've taken you somewhere quick, and we would've ended up at a hotel where I would be breaking your back by now," I said.

"Hello, I'm Mona. I'll be your waitress for the evening. I can take your drink orders while you look over the menu."

"Yes, I'll take a double Tito's and cranberry juice," Serenity said.

"I'll take a double Crown and sprite," I replied.

"Great. Would you like and appetizers?"

"I'll take the stuffed mushrooms," Serenity replied.

"Yeah, let me get the BBQ shrimp."

"I'll put your order in for your drinks and your appetizers," Mona said.

"So what made you want to become a social worker?" I asked.

"I always wanted to help children. I grew up with kids whose parents would abuse them or barely fed them, and I always was there to help them somehow," she replied.

I watched her as she talked about her love for being a social worker, and her whole face lit up when she did it.

"So what do you do for fun?" I asked.

"I hang out with my girls, Starr and Kash," she replied.

"Wait. Kashmir? The PR rep?" I asked.

"Yeah. That's one of my best friends," she replied.

"Get the hell out of here. That is my PR rep; she's on my team."

"Well, it's a small world," she replied.

THE WAITRESS RETUNED with our drinks. The vibe between Serenity and I was completely different than any other chick that I had been out with. They were more concerned with who I was messing with and what type of money I had that they didn't focus on Kyron the man; they focused on Smoove the entertainer. I could tell that she was a down to earth chick simply by the way that she carried herself, and it didn't hurt that she was friends with Kash either.

Our appetizers came out, I wasn't a big fan of mushrooms, but they looked good as hell sitting on her plate. She noticed that I was looking at them with my mouth watering and started to laugh.

"Would you like one, Kyron?" she asked.

"Hell yeah, they ain't never looked so good before."

She pushed her plate over to me so that I could grab some. Then I offered some of my shrimp, and we continued to talk. By the time that our entrée came, we had been talking for what felt like hours. We ate some of our meal and asked to have it boxed up because she had to go get her son and I had to head back to the studio for a session with another artist. I took her back to the studio, where she left her car. When she got out, I wrapped my arms around her waist. I don't know why I did it, it just felt natural, and she didn't put up a fight.

"I enjoyed your company tonight," she said.

"I did too. What you doing tomorrow?" I asked.

"I'm not sure what I have planned once I get off. What's up?" she asked.

"I'm not sure yet. I'll hit you up," I replied.

As she walked around to the driver's side of the car, I followed her. She went to say something, and I couldn't resist kissing her sweet, soft lips. Kissing had never been my thing, but I just had to feel them and good lord I didn't want to pull away.

"Well, that was unexpected," she said.

"I'm sorry. I been wanting to do that all night," I replied.

After talking a couple more minutes, I watched as she drove off after telling me that she will text me when she makes it home. I walked into the studio to work on this track, but my mind was on Serenity. Damn, just from a kiss she got my head fucked up.

9

Kashmir

"Oh my, this your house?" I asked.

"Yeah, this is one of the many houses that I have. In fact this is the only one that I didn't put on the market," he replied.

I was completely amazed at the house that was sitting in front of me. It was sitting on about three acres of land with no one around for about a good ten minutes. It was beautifully built with floor to ceiling windows at the front of the house. As he backed his car into the garage and popped the trunk, I waited for him to come around and open my door.

"Go ahead in; the garage door is open."

I walked into the house to a large open floor plan with a view of a lake through the sliding glass doors. I walked to the doors and went outside. It was so quiet that you could hear the crickets outside.

"Would you like something to drink? There is water, beer, soda in the fridge," he said.

"I'm okay right now."

"Make yourself comfortable, I'm going to unpack the trunk and handle a couple things real quick," he said.

I wasn't in a rush to head back to the city anyway. I walked into the kitchen, grabbed a water and turned on the TV. By the time that Karter finished whatever he was doing, I was hungry as hell.

"Karter," I called.

I didn't get a response from him, so I ventured off into the house to find him. Looking into all of the rooms, which was about five, I came to the last room that had the door opened.

"Karter," I called again before walking into the room.

As I made my way into the bedroom, Karter walked out of the bathroom with a towel wrapped around his waist and his earbuds in his ears. When he saw that I was standing there, he pulled one of the buds out. Meanwhile, I was staring at his dick print that was showing through the towel, and I was impressed

"I'm sorry. What's up?" he asked.

"I was coming to see if you were hungry, because I am. Do you want me to order something?" I asked,

"Yeah, I'm hungry. Give me a minute and I'll be right down," he said.

I turned on my heels fast as hell and speed-walked out of the room. I was halfway down the hall when he called me.

"Kash?" he said.

"Yeah," I replied, turning around.

He stood there smirking with the towel still wrapped around his waist.

"This ain't what you want in your life, sweetheart. I promise you that it will have you wide open," he smirked.

"Yeah whatever," I replied.

When I got downstairs, I went straight to the bar area; I needed something to take the edge off from being around him. He came downstairs in about ten minutes with some ball shorts on with a tank and some slides.

"I had the groundskeeper go to the store for me because I knew that I would be up here soon. She brought some steaks and shrimp that I could throw on the grill if you wanted to go ahead and make a side or two to go with it."

"Yeah, I can do that. Let me see what you have in here," I replied.

I walked into the kitchen to see what I could whip up real quick. He had a little bit of everything, but I settled on a salad and some bacon-wrapped asparagus. Karter turned on some music and fired up the grill.

"Kash, do you mind making me a Henny on the rocks?!" he yelled in the house.

When I was finished, I went to the bar, made his drink, and took it to him. I sat down at the patio table and sipped on my drink while he cooked.

"So Karter, tell me what that was all about before we came up here?"

"That was my soon-to-be ex-wife, Bailee. We are recently separated, and she hasn't come to grips with it yet."

"Well, how recent are we talking about?"

"Today make two days," he replied.

"Do you mind if I ask what happened?"

"Bailee wanted to continue living the lifestyle that landed me in prison for a couple years. When I was locked down, I told her that once I got out, I was making some changes and that it would be wise for her to go with it. Well, she didn't want to hear it. In fact, while I was down, she was carrying herself like she didn't have a husband that had eyes and ears everywhere."

"So she cheated?" I asked.

"It's possible she did; I wouldn't put it past her. So when I got out, I gave it six months hoping that she would come around, which she didn't, and here we are."

"That's rough."

"Now tell me about this nigga that can't take a breakup. You must got that thang if he throwing bricks and shit through expensive ass windows and shit."

"I'm not sure what you mean by that thang, but I was just tired of his bullshit. He had two kids on me already, and another one just came to my door talking about she pregnant by him. I have had enough. It's time for me to move on to someone that will love me the right way," I said.

"I hear you, ma."

We sat on the patio and traded stories about our upbringing. I found out that his parents are still happily married, and that Karter had twin daughters, Paris and London. I told him about how I wanted to start my own PR firm, and he told me that I should go for it because my name alone carried a lot of weight. We sat out on the patio and ate dinner. Once we finished dinner, we cleaned the kitchen and decided on waiting until the morning to head back to the city.

"Do you want to shower? We can wash what you have on so it will be fresh," he asked.

"Yeah, that sounds like a plan."

"You can shower in my room; I'll give you something to sleep in."

I followed him into his room where he pulled out a t-shirt and a pair of baller shorts. When I walked into the bathroom and started the shower, there was a knock on the door.

"Here is some of the girl's shower gel. I know you don't want to smell all manly and shit," he said, handing it to me.

I stepped into the shower. The water was warm, and he had one of the double-headed showerheads, something that I had been planning on getting for my bathroom. I swear it felt like I had been in the shower forever. When I came out of the bathroom, Karter was lounging in the bed watching TV smoking a blunt.

"Do you want to watch TV here or in the theater?" he asked.

"It doesn't matter to me, here is fine."

I walked to the other side of the bed and got myself comfortable on top of the sheets. I didn't want him to get the wrong idea; it was bad enough that I was in his bedroom with his clothes on.

Karter got up out the bed and left the room, returning a couple minutes later with drinks that he had made for him and I with a comforter for me to use.

"I figured that you wouldn't want to be under the covers with me, so I brought you this," he explained, handing me the blanket.

We turned on Netflix and watched a couple movies until our eyes got heavy. I didn't plan on sleeping in his bed, I was going to go the guest room and sleep, but my body wouldn't let me move out of the bed.

When I woke up the next morning, Karter wasn't in bed. I walked into the bathroom to wash my face and relieve myself when I noticed that there was an unopened toothbrush sitting on the counter. I could smell the bacon that was being cooked from downstairs. I made my way downstairs to find Karter in the kitchen with no shirt on making breakfast.

"Good morning," I said.

"Good morning, Kash. How did you sleep?"

"That bed is amazing; I need to get me one."

I was trying to keep my eyes from falling below his chest because him standing there with no shirt on, with his chiseled stomach and his shorts hanging low, was doing something to me.

"You want some coffee or something?" he asked.

"If you point me to the stuff, I'm pretty sure that I would make it."

He showed me where the stuff for the coffee was while he finished cooking.

"Kash, can I ask you a question?"

"Yeah, go ahead."

"Do I turn you on?"

I damn near choked on my coffee because I wasn't expecting that question to be asked. I had to think long and hard before I answer this question.

"No, you don't turn me on," I lied.

"Okay." Was his response, and he went back to cooking.

"So, if I do this, you don't feel anything?" he asked, standing behind me closely

"Not a thing," I replied.

"You're lying but okay."

He made our plates, and the only thing that you could hear was the forks hitting the plate. I guess both of us were hungry or maybe we were trying to avoid conversation. As we were eating, Kyron's assistant called asking when was a good time to have interviews for new security. I was telling her to get with Karter, when he snatched the phone from me and told her that he had a meeting later this afternoon and he was talking care of everything.

"I was going to tell you when we finished about the meeting."

"It's fine. Let me go clean this kitchen up and you go get dressed," I said.

"It's cool. Someone is coming to clean the house today anyway," he replied.

We got dressed and headed back to the city. As much as I wanted to stay at the house, I knew that I had to come back to handle business and get my house in order. I was deep in thought when Karter's phone rang. He connected it to the car radio.

"What's up?

"Nigga, where you been?" the voice asked.

"Pops, I been up at the lake house."

"Come by the house a little later," the voice said.

"Ok, I'll be there," he replied.

When we arrived back at the house, I really didn't want to go inside. I wanted to stay in his presence. I got out of the car after agreeing that I would get with him once I got the windows and stuff take care of.

Karter

MY EVENING with Kash was something that I hadn't had in a long time. It was nothing but peaceful and relaxing. Even with me cooking dinner, which was actually something that I like doing but with Bailee, she took the joy out it when I did cook. It was like her, and I just vibe together, and it was something that I was really feeling. I wanted to test the waters with her, especially after she didn't stop me from kissing her.

When I dropped her off, she seemed reluctant to leave me, and that made a nigga feel good. I had to go by Kyron's house and scoop him so that we could meet up with his new security team. I called him to let him know to come outside because I wasn't in the mood to wait. When I pulled up to his building, he was talking to the security guard outside. He got into the car and I pulled off.

"What's up with you?" he asked.

"Shit, just came back from the lake house. What about you?"

"Nothing much. Went to the studio and met this lil' baddie that know Kash," he replied.

'What you mean, knows Kash?" I asked.

"She says that they are best friends."

"Oh word? Maybe that is what you need, a friend like Kash that will keep your ass in check."

We pulled up to the restaurant where we were meeting the security company. I was referred to them by one of my contacts in Texas, and they said that they were legit. The owner of the company is a former Navy Seal, and he is all about business. I pulled into the valet and got out. After telling the valet not to scratch my shit, we told the hostess our name and waited to be seated. I had reserved a small dining room so that we could conduct our meeting without everyone being around.

We were led to our area, and we waited for the other party to arrive. We had gotten here about ten minutes before the meeting was to start, because I wanted to see what type of man he was. Was he one of those that arrived right on time? Or would he arrive a couple minutes early? After about a minute or so, the hostess brought back two men.

"Mr. Sterling, I'm Rashad, and this is my brother Jahlid," he said, extending his hand.

"Nice to meet you. I'm Karter, and this is Kyron," I informed.

We sat down and got to business. I told them the type of security team that I was looking for. I wanted someone that was going to be the eyes and ears for me when I was and wasn't there.

"I see that you got into a little scuffle the other night," Rashad said.

"Yeah, it was a fucked-up situation with my baby momma," Kyron replied.

"Do you mind me asking where security was?" Jahlid asked.

"Hell, they prolly was hanging with the chicks at the bar," Kyron said.

"That's rule number one. We don't leave our client unattended," Jahlid said.

"I heard that your PR person was Kash," Rashad said.

"Yeah, she is," Kyron.

Just the thought of another man mentioning Kash's name was making me feel some kind of way, but I know that I shouldn't because I hadn't even smelled the pussy yet. I told them that I wanted to do a trial run with them tonight to see how they would handle the different things that could come about when Kyron would do club appearances. We agreed that we would meet tonight at Kyron's house and head out to a few clubs. They were my clubs, so I knew that we were good, but they didn't need to know that.

No sooner than I got out of the restaurant, I received a call from my security company letting me know that the silent alarm was triggered at the house on Broad Street. We got into the car and peeled out of the parking lot heading that way. When I pulled up the house, there was fire trucks everywhere, and it was taped off. I jumped out the car with it still running and went to talk to the officer.

"What the fuck is going on with my house?" I asked.

"Sir, we responded to a call from the alarm company. When we got here, there was a small fire in the back of the house in the kitchen. We dispatched the fire department. Do you know if anyone was in the house?" the officer asked.

"Nah, the house was up for sale, so no one was staying in it," I replied.

As we were talking, the Lieutenant walked over to us.

"Are you the owner of the house?" He asked.

"Yes, that is me."

"Do you know how the fire started in the kitchen?" he asked.

"No, I was in a meeting when I received the call. I hadn't even been here in months," I replied.

"Well, it appears to be arson. We will have an investigator contact you about the investigation," he replied.

"Were you able to put the fire out?" I questioned.

"Yes, we were able to put it out. There is some fire and water damage to the kitchen, but the rest of the house is still intact," he responded.

I walked to the back of the house and it was black shit and water all over the kitchen. I was mad as shit trying to figure who would do something like this to my house. Just as I was walking back to my car, Bailee's ass called.

"Yeah?"

"Don't sound too happy to hear from me?" she replied sarcastically.

"What's up, man?"

"Did you and your new bitch have fun last night?" she asked.

"Now is not the time to be playing with me, what you want?"

"I was calling because I got a call about one of the houses; the alarm company called," she replied.

Which that was a lie because the company was to call me first and if they couldn't reach me, they were to call my pops.

"Yep everything straight," I lied.

"Oh okay, that is all that I wanted," she said with an attitude.

Hanging up from her, I looked at Kyron and shook my head. In the back of my mind, I wondered if she had something to do with the fire at the house.

"What lil' bitch, B talking about?" Kyron asked.

"It was Kash; we stopped by the hotel yesterday to get some stuff. We had plans to go back to her house after that nigga broke her windows and shit but instead, we headed up to the lake house and chilled," I said.

"Ahhh shit. You about to fuck this whole thing up, nigga," he said.

"Why you say that?" I asked.

"Kash isn't your typical chick. She isn't impressed by the money; she's a real deal boss," he said.

"Anyway, what time you want to head out?"

"Let's go about twelve," he responded.

I dropped my brother off and headed to meet up with Shyne. I had got word that we were receiving a new shipment of product and I wanted everyone to be on their toes with this one. It was something about the way the connect was speaking that had me on high alert.

When I pulled up to his house, he was standing outside with two chicks; one of them was his baby moms Sabrina and the other I assumed was his jump-off. I jumped out of the car because it looked like he had his hands full trying to keep them from kicking each other's ass.

"Aye man, grab one of these broads!" he yelled.

I walked over and lifted Sabrina's ass up, kicking and screaming as she made threats to kick the chick and Shyne's ass. Sitting her ass down by the car, I gave her ass a look that told her don't play with me and she stood there.

"Calm the fuck down with all that rah-rah. Where my nephew anyway?" I asked.

"He with my homegirl, I just came over here because I needed some money. I knock on the door, and this dirty dick nigga got that flat-chested bitch laying on the couch and shit."

"Ya baby daddy like it though," the other chick yelled.

As Shyne told the other chick to go inside and get dressed so she can bounce, I gave Sabrina a couple hundred and told her to leave. I also told her that she betta spend some on my nephew or her ass won't get another dime from me. When she pulled off, I had to shake my head at the craziness that Shyne had going on.

"What's up, boss?" He asked.

"For one, you need to get your shit in order; having women fighting outside of your spot isn't a good look. You need to make that shit clear with Brina that is it a wrap so she can move the fuck on and not try to fight every chick that she sees you with. Now, that I got that out of the way, your men ready for the shipment tonight?" I asked.

"Yeah, everyone knows the time and place to meet up," he replied.

"Good. Tell those niggas to keep their eyes and ears open at all time. This is a new shipment and new product, so I don't want no fuck-ups," I said.

"I got you. Everyone knows the deal if they fuck up," he replied.

"We sliding through Karma tonight to see how this new security company will work with Kyron. Once everything is secure and in order, slide through. They're having a couple acts perform tonight."

"Bet. I'll be there," he replied.

I got back in my whip, headed to grab me something to eat from King's and headed to the hotel to relax. Pops could wait 'til later. I got to King's and ordered me a fish platter with extra-large shrimp, a side of hush puppies and coleslaw. While I was waiting on my food, Loud ass Tara came in with her equally loud ass friends. I was sitting in the corner looking down at my phone, hoping that these chicks wouldn't come my way.

"Oh, girl, isn't that your baby daddy fine ass brother?" One of the chicks asked.

"Yes, that my brother-in-law that's married to my cousin," Tara replied.

"Married? Word on the street is he left Bailee ass," the other chick said.

"Chile, believe what you want. His ass will be back just like Kyron will be back."

BOTH OF THE chicks started laughing at Tara. I guess she didn't find it funny because when I looked up, she looked like someone shitted in her food as hard as she had her face screwed up. I was glad when they called my number because I didn't want to sit there a minute longer than I had to. I grabbed my food, gave their ass 'what's up' nod, and bounced. It took me about fifteen minutes to get to the hotel, and once I got to the room, I took off my shirt, watch and shoes in order to smash my food. My food was still nice and hot, so I poured myself some Henny on the rocks and went to work on my food.

Once I finished my food, I found something to wear; this was the first time that I had stepped out as a separated man. I wasn't looking to find someone to take home because that wasn't my steelo, but I wanted to look fresh. I called my barber to have him come cut me up once he was finished with his last client.

Kyron

"Nisha, call Tara ass and see if I can get KJ tomorrow 'til Sunday," I said into the phone.

"Okay, I'll text you want she said. Now I'm letting you know; if she tries to pop shit, I'm going straight to her house. I'm sick of her fake bad and bougie ass," Tara said.

"Ight, Nisha. You damn sure don't need another case on your ass," I laughed.

I was sitting in the living room listening to a couple tracks that one of my producers sent over. I was working on material for my album release. I had plans to perform four or five songs and let the rest just be played. Once we had that taken care of, we were heading out on a promo tour where I was the opening act for a big headliner. I was in my zone when Tara hardheaded ass started calling. I sent her to voicemail, and she sent a text. I ignored that, and it seemed like she was going back and forth between the two. So I finally answered the phone after the hundredth call.

"What, man?"

"I don't appreciate you having your lil' flunkies calling me trying to make arrangements about our son," she said.

"Yo, I told your ass the other day that I was going through her or mom, so come on now," I replied.

"KJ will be going with my mom this week so you gotta ask her can you get KJ."

"Come again? I gotta ask your mom's permission to get my child? Look, I'm not about to play these games with you. So check it, I'm going to have my lawyer draw up some child support and visitation agreement because I don't have the time or energy to play these childish ass games with you," I replied and hung up.

Tara had my mood all the way fucked up, so I texted Serenity to see what she was doing because she sure as hell didn't text me like I asked her last night.

Me: I'm going to assume you made it home safely? Lol.

Serenity: Omg! I completely forgot, please forgive me.

Me: Only because you're so beautiful.

Serenity: What you doing? At the studio?

Me: Nah, I'm home listening to some tracks. I'm heading out to make a quick appearance at this club later on.

Serenity: I'll be in the house unless I get dragged out of the house or something.

Me: Cool. I gotta make a few calls; I'll hit you up in a bit.

I NEEDED to lay down because the drama with Tara had my head hurting. I had a lot of things going on and battling her to see my son was the last thing that I wanted to do. I smoked me a blunt while watching TV until I dozed off. If it wasn't for my momma coming into my house with all that noise, I probably would've been sleep.

"Hey, baby," she said.

"What's up, Dukes?" I replied.

"I just came over here real quick to drop some of this food off that I cooked today, your daddy wanted some Gumbo, so I whipped it up," she replied, placing the bags on the counter.

"Word, I'm about to smash that right now. What else you got in that bag?" I asked.

"I wrapped up a couple of your favorites, all you have to do is turn the oven on and put them in to heat up," she replied.

"Bet. I appreciate it, ma."

"Anything for my babies. What you got planned for later?" she asked.

"Karter and I are going out tonight to see how this new security team will work out with me and the crowds that come around, kind of like a test run."

"Well, y'all be careful out there. I'll talk to you tomorrow." She kissed me and walked out of the door.

. . .

I LOOKED AT THE CLOCK, and I had a couple hours to get ready. I needed a shave and an edge, so I called our barber and told him to come through. He informed me that he was going to Karter's to cut him up and just to meet him there. I figured that I would just grab my clothes and stuff for tonight and get dressed in Karter's room.

As I was leaving out to head over there, the security called me and told me that Tara's ass was at the desk trying to come up. I told them not to let her up, and I would be down. She was working all of my nerves, especially with this popping up and shit at my spot; she knows that I don't move like that.

By the time I made it downstairs, she was yelling and screaming like she was a maniac.

"I CAN'T BELIEVE YOU GOT ME OUT HERE STANDING LIKE I'M A FUCKING BUM ON THE STREET!" Tara yelled.

"Man, what's up?" I asked.

"I need some money; KJ needs milk and pampers," she replied.

"That's a lie, try again," I replied.

My son just had a delivery sent today with his formula and pampers along with some clothes and shoes.

"Look, I think that you should just give me some money for my needs because I have your son," she replied.

"Wrong. I take care of my son, so that means that you should be taken care of yourself. I'm not about to support you when you can't show me that you can hold your own."

"But you can support all these hoes out here in the street though? I heard about the chick you was with," she replied.

"One, the only hoe that I ever dated was you, and you didn't start out like that. Two, what I do with my money that I work hard for is none of your concern. Three, if you don't like it, do something about it. I tried to be fair when it came to my son, but you want to act like he is a pawn in a game and I ain't having it, so like I said, I'll get the papers drawn up," I responded, walking away.

I don't why Tara was making this harder than this needed to

be. I was only giving her money to support our son, and that was it. All that other shit that she was talking about I wasn't trying to hear it. I jumped into my Gunmetal Gray Range Rover and headed to my brother's hotel room. I forgot to tell him that I was on the way so I decided that I would hit him up real quick.

"What's up?" he answered.

"Yo, I'm coming to your room to get me a cut, it makes no sense for him to come to you than me when I can just come over," I said.

"Nigga, you acting like we about to have a slumber party and shit."

"Man, shut your frog-headed ass up. I'll see you in a few," I said, hanging up.

It took me about thirty minutes to get to Karter's room, and when I got there, he was already sitting in the chair getting a haircut. I went over to the bar, poured me a drink and turned to Sports Center. I had brought the gumbo that ma had brought over and put in the microwave to warm up.

"I know this nigga didn't bring him something to eat and didn't bring me none. Hold up, is that Ma's gumbo?" he asked.

I nodded my head because I was trying to savor every bit of the flavors.

"I should knock that shit out of your hand for not bringing me none," he said.

"Here, crybaby ass," I said, taking the rest of the food out of the bag.

"Yeah, cause I was about to call moms. She tripping just bringing you food and didn't call me," he said.

It took us about two hours to get ready, and that was because we was fucking off, playing the game, having drinks and smoking cigars just chilling. The security knocked on the door and let us know that they were ready to move. I was impressed because you couldn't tell that was security, they looked just like one of the homies. One was dressed in Gucci with the shoes to match, and the other had on Balmain with a pair of fresh wheat color Timb's. We stepped out of the hotel to the waiting Black Benz Sprinter that they had waiting for us.

"Okay, I see how y'all do. Good look, Jahlid and Rashad," I said.

"No doubt. We in the big boy league's around here," Jahlid said.

When we got in, they had the AC blasting, and the music was playing. Jahlid and Rashad sat in the back with us while their other brother drove.

"See, our company is a family business, I employ my family and close friends to work with me," Rashad said.

The ride to the club was about thirty minutes. We sat back and had a couple more drinks, while Jahlid and Karter talked about various things. When we pulled to the front of the club, it was like a scene out of a movie, all waiting on ya boy. It was Karter's club, but I was a local celebrity, so when people heard that I was coming through, the whole city turned out.

"Aight, so we are going to get out and clear the area first, make sure that no one can grab on you or nothing like that. Now, if you want to sign autographs that is on you, but we will keep a close eye on you. I already spoke with the manager of the club so we will be going up the back steps to get to your VIP section and then we can vibe from there," Jahlid said.

I was already impressed at the level of professionalism that they were displaying right now. In my book, they were hired, but it was Karter's decision at the end of the day.

10

Kashmir

"YOU BETTER BE lucky that I didn't have anything to do tonight or your ass would've been here by yourself," Serenity fussed as we walked to our table.

"Girl, hush. You know you would've come even if you did have something because you love me," I replied.

"Can I take your order?' the waitress asked.

"Yes, I'll take a Patron and pineapple. What you want, Serenity?" I yelled over the music.

"Oh, can I get a leg spreader?" Serenity stated.

"Put this on Dre and tell him Kash is here," I said to the waitress.

THE ONLY REASON I came out tonight was because my college friend asked me to come check out some of the acts tonight. They were having a showcase, and he was the promoter of this event.

"Girl, what you and Dre got going on?" Serenity asked.

"Not a damn thing. He asked me to come check out some acts

because he knows that I'm connecting in the music industry," I replied.

"Oh, so girl, let me tell you. Why I went out on a date last night," Serenity said.

"Hold up! Stop the presses! Who is this, man?" I asked.

Just as Serenity was about to say something, there was a bunch of yelling and clapping. We looked up to see Kyron standing in the VIP overlooking the crowd. I was in complete awe of Karter, who was standing next to him dripping with swag. Much like the other times that I had seen him, he was dressed in Gucci top to bottom, but this time, he was sporting a hat and was sexy as hell. He had a diamond chain around his neck that shined brightly along with his Rolex. I was a watch girl and could spot one a mile away.

"Earth to Serenity!" I yelled over the music.

"Oh, what was I saying?" she asked.

"You were about to tell me who this mystery man was."

"He's not a mystery."

Before I could ask her what she was talking about, I smelled the familiar cologne that only one person could wear the hell out of.

"Good evening, ladies," Karter said.

"Hello, Karter," I replied.

"Who's the beautiful women sitting next to you?" He asked.

"This is one of my best friends, Serenity."

"Nice to meet you," Serenity said.

"So look we're up in the VIP, why don't y'all join us," he stated.

"I'm here checking out a couple act, maybe later," I replied.

"Okay. Handle your business then," he said.

I felt the disappointment in his response, and Serenity was staring at me like I had two heads because I turned his offer down. She was down my throat as soon as he walked away.

"Girl, we could've been popping bottles up in VIP," she said.

"We will a little later but tell me who this mystery man is?"

"Not right now because it was just one date, but if things change, I will let you know."

Our drinks came, and we began to watch the acts. Some of them were really good and could go places if they mastered their craft. Serenity and I was on our second drink when we got up to use the bathroom. On my way, I was snatched back by my arm. When I turned around, there was Gio with a look of anger on his face.

"So this is how you doing it? Hanging out in the clubs and shit like you a hot girl?"

"First, get your fucking hands off me. Second, we aren't together, so I don't have to answer to you about shit, and finally, I suggest you get the fuck out of my face after you did that shit to my house," I said.

Before he could get anything out of his mouth, there stood Karter with two other guys.

"We got a problem here?" he asked, staring at me.

"Nah, my dude. I was just talking to my girl," Gio replied.

"I'm not your girl, and no, we do not have a problem,"

"So, it looks like the woman doesn't want to talk to you, my man, so why don't you just walk it off?" Karter said.

"Nigga, who the fuck is you? I told you that I was talking to my lady so what you need to do is mind your fucking business before we have a problem," Gio said.

"My dude, I promise you this ain't what you want," he said, walking into Gio's personal space.

The way that Karter was talking to Gio had my panties soaked. I wasn't sure if it was the way he handled the situation or the authoritative voice that he was giving off. Karter stood there waiting for Gio to decide on what move he wanted to make while he stared at me like he was undressing me with his eyes. Gio finally decided to take the hint and leave, and so did the guys that were with Karter.

"Sorry about that. I don't know why he doesn't take the hint."

"No need to apologize. I mean you are a beautiful, sexy woman who knows that he fucked up. Look, follow me and you can use my bathroom in my office."

"What do you mean, your office?" I asked.

"This is one of my establishments," he replied.

When we walked into his office, he had monitors all over the walls. There was a view of every angle, even the bathroom, and the halls. He showed me where the bathroom was, and I went in to relieve myself. I was shocked because it was super clean even for it to be in a club. There was a shower inside the bathroom with a closet that had clothes inside. When I returned into the office, he was leaning up against his desk looking at the monitors with his arms crossed.

"Thank you," I replied.

Standing up from his desk, he walked so close into my personal space that I could smell the spearmint gum on his breath.

"You are making this working relationship harder and harder each time that I see you," he stated.

"I'm not sure what you mean."

"This dress that you are wearing, these heels and your perfume."

I knew what he meant because he turned me the fuck on every time I saw him. With his lips so close to me I couldn't do anything but invite his lips onto mine. As we kissed deeply, passionately, he wrapped his arms around me while he walked me back to the couch. Turning around, he sat in the chair, causing me to straddle him with my dress now above my waist and my ass fully exposed. I could feel his manhood rise as our kiss deepened. We were so into it that we didn't hear anything until someone started yelling.

"I know you aren't in here getting your dick wet while I'm home with our daughters," the woman yelled.

Breaking away from our kiss, Karter lifted me up and placed me on my feet as he kissed me again before I walked off to the bathroom.

"Is this the same bitch from the other day?" she asked.

"What the fuck are you doing here, Bailee?" Karter asked.

"I came here because I wanted to talk to you, but I see that you would rather get your dick wet by your little bitch in there," she yelled.

I walked out the bathroom because I had enough of her and the name calling, but before I said anything, Karter was handling it.

"Bailee, there ain't shit for us to talk about, I thought I made that shit clear the day I left. Watch what you say about people because this woman right here damn sure ain't no bitch or a chick that I'm fucking," he said.

"I can leave so you guys can talk," I interrupted.

"Nah, Kash, you straight. Bailee was just leaving," Karter said.

There I was standing in the bathroom thinking to myself how I was just slobbing the manager of one of my clients like it was nobody's business. Thank God Bailee walked in when she did because who knows how far we would've went.

"That's fine. Sweetie, you can stay here with my husband but trust me, he will come back. I'm his first love, something that even you can't replace," she said.

The whole time that she was talking, Karter was texting someone on the phone. The next thing I knew two dudes came into the office and walked Bailee out. Karter watched while the other chicks that came with her was rounded up and escorted out of the club.

"Kash, excuse me for like twenty minutes, baby. Go head down and order whatever you and Serenity want on me," Karter spoke.

"Don't worry about it, I already have the drinks covered from the promoter," I replied, walking out the door.

"KASH!" he yelled.

Turning back onto my heels, I walked back inside.

"Yes?"

"You and Serenity are being moved, and we won't talk about that. I apologize for what happened with Bailee there," he said, walking over to me and kissing me gently.

When I pulled back from the kiss, the security was coming down the hall. They entered the office and closed the door. When I made it back downstairs, someone was waiting on me.

"Are you Kash?" the guy asked.

"Yes."

"Follow me. I'm Jahlid, one of Smoove's security guards," he said.

Following behind him, we walked right up to where Kyron and Serenity were. It looked like the two of them was in a deep conversation because they stopped when we entered the section.

"Well, what's going on here?' I asked.

"Kash, so you know the dude I went on a date with?" she asked.

"Yeah.... Oh shit! It was Kyron?" I asked.

They both looked at each other, then back to me and shook they head.

"Well, y'all grown but Kyron, don't mess over my bestie," I replied.

After about thirty minutes or so, Karter returned to our section. Dre texted me to see where I was at, and I let him know that I was in the VIP section. He said that he would call me tomorrow to see how I liked the acts, so I told him to call me at the office after ten. For the remainder of the night, we had a couple more drinks, and when it was time for the club to close, we still didn't leave. We sat around for another hour or so enjoying the music and just chilling. I knew that I had work to do in the morning, so I told Serenity that I was ready to leave. Kyron said that I could leave and he would make sure that she got home safely.

"Can I catch a ride with you back to the hotel?" Karter asked.

"Sure," I replied.

As we left out of the club, I reached into my purse to get my keys. Once they were in my hand, Karter took them from me and unlocked the door, walking me to the passenger side to let me in.

"You do know that this is my car and I'm very capable of driving?" I stated.

"I know, sweetheart, but you are in the presence of a real man. When we are together, I do all of that," he replied and closed my door.

We pulled out of the parking lot and drove to Ihop. I didn't notice that I was hungry until he pulled up. When we walked into the restaurant, Karter told the hostess that we needed a table while I went and washed my hands and got myself together. By the time that I made it back out, he was already seated looking over the menu. I got into the booth and waited until the waitress arrived. I already knew what I wanted to eat.

. . .

"HELLO, can I start you guys off with something to drink?" the waitress asked.

"Yes, I'll just take a sprite, and I know what I want. Do you know what you want?" Karter asked.

"Yes, I'm ready to order," I replied.

The waitress took our order, and then there was this awkward silence cause both of us were busy in our phones. I wanted to say something but didn't know what to say or if it would even make it more awkward. Placing his phone down, Karter stared at me waiting for me to finish what I was doing.

"Be honest with me real quick," Karter said.

"About what?"

"Do I make you nervous?" he asked.

"Why do you keep asking me that?"

"Because I can read body language and your body is telling me everything that I need to know but, in order for any of this to work, I need you to be honest and upfront with me."

"Do I make you nervous, Karter?"

"Nervous? Nah, turned on like a motherfucker but definitely not nervous. Like you sitting there with that tight ass dress on and them titties sitting up right got me on brick."

"I don't make it a habit of mixing business with pleasure."

"I hear what your mouth says but your body tells me something else."

Before I could respond, the waitress brought our food and thank God that she did because this conversation was going in a direction that I knew if we continued, we would end up in the back of my car like a bunch of teenagers. As Karter ate his food, I watched as he devoured it and began to fantasize about his lips devouring my pearl. It has been months since my sexual appetite had been filled.

"You don't like your food?" Karter asked.

"Oh it's good," I replied, shaking the thoughts I had out of my head.

We finished eating our food, and Karter paid the bill while I went and washed my hands. Standing in the mirror, I had to go give myself a little pep talk before going back out.

Get it together, girl. Yes, he is fione, but this isn't the first fine ass man that you have been around. Yes, you want to rip his clothes off, but this is your client's brother. Keep it professional.

Walking out of the bathroom, Karter was standing at the door waiting on me to come. He held the door for me to exit the restaurant and the door for me to get back into the car. He had Tank's radio playing as we made our way back to the hotel.

I like it when you lose it
I like it when you go there
I like the way you use it
I like that you don't play fair
Recipe for a disaster
When I'm just tryna take my time
Stroke is gettin' deep and faster
You're screamin' like I'm outta line

THE COMBINATION OF TANK PLAYING, his damn cologne and me being tipsy still was taking a toll on me. I was praying to God that he would hurry up and get us to the hotel so that I could get the hell away from him before I jumped over this seat and straddled him. As we pulled into the hotel, I waiting for the Valet to open the door so I could speed walk to the elevators. I was trying to get away from Karter, but he was right on my ass.

We got onto the elevator and made it to our floor, I fumbled to find my key inside my purse.

"You straight over there?" Karter asked, leaning against the wall.

"Yes, I found my key," I replied.

Unlocking the door, I walked into the room and kicked off my shoes. Karter followed behind me.

"I'm going to sit your keys right here okay," he said.

"Thank you," I replied.

"Alright. I'll holla atchu' in the morning. Be easy," he said and closed the door behind him.

I was in complete shock before I knew like hell that he was about to try something. Shaking it off, I started the shower and took off my makeup. I still couldn't get the vision of him and I in the office tonight out of my head. As I dried off and put my pajamas on, I climbed into bed and closed my eyes.

11

Karter

Kash has no idea how much restraint I was practicing right now. That little incident in my office was nothing compared to what I really wanted to do to her. As I paced back and forth in my room with a drink in my hand, I went back and forth on whether I should go and knock on her door or leave her alone. I was a savage when it came to sex, so I knew that once I touched the kitty, it would be over. I knew that she didn't want to mix business with pleasure, so I was going to respect that until she made up her mind that she was going to accept being my lady.

It was going on four in the morning, and I was wide awake watching TV. I had some pent up stress that I needed to relive. As I was scrolling through my phone to see who I could unleash on, there was a knock at the door. Setting my phone down, I walked to the door without looking into the peephole. I got the shock of my life when I opened the door, and there stood Kash in a pair of booty shorts and a cami. Her hair was hanging past her shoulder.

"Did I wake you?" she asked.

Raising my glass, she caught my drift, walking into the room uninvited. The sexual tension between us was so thick that you could cut it with a knife.

"Can I help you with something?" I asked, closing the door.

She didn't say a word, just went to untie the pajama pants that I was wearing.

"Woah, you sure you want to do this? There is no turning back from this, Kash," I said, staring dead in her eyes, holding onto her hands.

She stared at me, not saying a word, but I wanted to be clear that she understood that I wasn't with the games or even sharing.

"I need you to tell me that you understand."

"Yes, I understand you, Karter," she replied.

That was music to my ears as I let her hands go, and she finished untying my pants. She put her hands inside to feel this long rod that was awaiting her. It has been a minute since I had been inside something warm and wet. We engaged in a passionate kiss while she pulled my pants down, and I just stepped out of them. I removed her top and lifted her, so she was now straddling me as I walked into the bedroom.

Lying her down in the bed, I remove her tiny boy shorts that she was wearing to reveal her bald pussy. She sat up on her elbows to look at me while my mouth watered looking at her fully nude. I lowered myself to my knees as I got eye level with her glistening pussy. I blew on it and she began to squirm. Spreading her lips, I began to suck on her pearl. As soon as I locked onto her, she began to run.

"Don't run, enjoy the ride," I said.

Locking her legs around my forearms so she couldn't go anywhere, I went in for the kill.

"Wait! Oh shit!" Kash said.

What she didn't know was the more vocal she was, the more I was turned on.

"Wait, Karter. I'm about to cum."

"Do that shit, baby," I said as I smacked her pussy.

As I went back to work, her legs began to shake, and she covered her face to keep her screams muffled while she came. I gave her a minute to catch her breath.

"How you want this dick? You can get it from the back, side, front, or all of them. Either way, I'm fucking up your walls tonight," I stated.

Kash shocked the shit out of me when she turned around and gave me the perfect arch in her back. As I entered her, I felt like I was in heaven; she was so warm and wet.

"Yeah, you done fucked up now," I said.

I dug in deeper because I wanted her to get the full effect of what I was giving her. I wanted her to be able to feel me inside of her when she walked.

"Damn," she said.

"Yeah, you ain't fucking with no lil' boy here, one hundred percent all man," I replied.

The only thing that could be heard in the room was Kash moaning and our skin slapping against each other. I was trying to delay the explosion that was building inside of me. I was doing good until Kash started throwing it back like she had lost her damn mind.

"Shit girl, it's like that?" I asked.

"Mmmmm. Just like that," she moaned.

KASH HAD the sexiest moan that I had ever heard. After about ten more minutes, I could no longer fight the urge.

"I'm about to cum," she said.

"Cum all on this dick, girl," I said.

As I looked down, the evidence of her creaming was visible everywhere on me.

"I'm cumming!" she yelled.

"Shit, I'm right there with you."

I emptied everything that was inside of me that was built up. It had been a minute since I had pussy good enough to make me cum like that. Bailee used to have some, but she got lazy when it came to the dick. Kash crawled up to the top of the bed and tried to catch her breath as she got under the covers. I got under also to catch my breath before I went in for round two.

I guess I dozed off in between catching my breath, cause I woke up to an empty bed. I got up to go relive myself and went to look for Kash. She wasn't anywhere in my room, so I figured that she had went to hers. I grabbed me a shirt and some shorts and headed over to her room only to be met by the housekeeping cleaning out her room.

"Where is the person that was staying in this room?" I asked.

"I have no idea, this room was on my list," the maid said.

Well damn, that's how Kash wanted to play this, I hope she remember what I told her because I wasn't with these teenage ass games. I was going to give her ass some time to think about things and then I'll holla at her.

I went back into my room to get myself showered and dressed for the day. I had a meeting with Nick to look at a couple condos and houses that he found. I was still pissed about the fire at one of my houses and had the word out to find out who was responsible for that. I had a feeling that Bailee had something to do with it, which I hoped and prayed she didn't.

I was walking out of the room when I received a call from a number I didn't recognize.

"Hello."

"Hello, Is this Mr. Sterling?" The voice asked.

"Yes, this is him."

"I'm Mico from Ms. Pitt's office calling to remind you of the strategy meeting that you all have today at two o'clock."

"Thank you. I will be there," I replied and hung up.

So that's how she wanted to do it? Fine with me. I went weeks and days without seeing people so it wouldn't hurt me.

By the time that I made it to Nick's office, he was standing outside talking on his phone. He walked over to the driver's side, and we switched. He knew where all the places were, so I didn't mind him pushing the whip. Once he finished up with his call, he stared off in the distance.

"What's up with you?" I asked.

"Man, that was Asia calling talking about she need more money."

Aisha was Nick's high school lil' boo. He would dip between her and Shanna until he settled down.

"What she need money for now because I know you paying that order."

"Man, I don't even ask," Nick replied.

We made it to the first condo. It was a tall building newly built with four bedrooms and three bathrooms. I walked through the condo, which had nice size bedrooms and bathrooms. The view was beautiful with the floor to ceiling windows.

"So what do you think?" Nick asked.

"It's cool, but I mean for three hundred thou, I need a hell of a lot more than this."

"I got a couple houses that we can check out," he replied.

"Yeah, let's do that," I stated, checking my watch.

The next three houses that Nick showed me was bad as hell and right up my alley. They had enough room for me and the girls plus more. All had large pools with grills, Jacuzzis, and a patio. One of the houses had a large man cave that piqued my interest after checking out the massive master bedroom and closet.

"Aye yo, Nick. I gotta make a move, let's ride," I announced.

We headed back to Nick's office where I told him to send over the information for the last house tonight, and I would get back to him. I had to head to this meeting for Kyron.

When I arrived at the location, Smoove and his assistant Nisha, Rashad and Jahlid were there. Kash had yet to get here, and there was a couple people from the label I assumed. Kash arrived after about seven or eight minutes with the same people that I saw at the hotel room before. She was wearing this navy-blue pants suit with a pink lace shirt that immediately had my man on hard.

"Good afternoon, everyone," she greeted us.

"Good afternoon," everyone responded.

I remained silent and just watched her conduct business.

"We are here today to come up with a plan of how we are going to get Mr. Sterling's career back on track. As you can see, Mr. Sterling has a new team. His brother Karter is his manager and Rashad and Jahlid run his new security team."

From there, we bounced around different ideas to get his image in a positive light. The meeting lasted about two hours, and when it was over, I walked out to the parking lot, got into my whip and headed to the girl's school. I promised that I would come and have lunch with them today.

12

Kyron

SOMETHING WAS GOING on with Karter and Kash. I watched as he stared at her the entire time at the meeting and she wouldn't even look at him. Kash was trying to play it off, but I knew my brother better than he thought. I even saw the way that he was watching her last night then disappeared and the next thing you know Kash is in our section, and he was acting like nothing happened. I was driving to Tara's house. I was going to get my son. She wasn't about to use my son as a fucking pawn in her little game that she wanted to play. I pulled up to her house, and she was sitting on the steps with her friends, smoking a blunt with a cup in her hand. I got out of my car and headed up the driveway.

"What you doing here?" she asked.

"I came here to get my son. The fuck you thought?"

"What you mean, come to get him?" she asked.

"I'm taking my son for a couple of days."

As soon as I walked into the house, I was disgusted by the smell and the crap that she had all over the floor. I could hear my son crying upstairs, and when I went into his room, it smelled like shit and piss.

"Yo man, what the fuck you got going on?"

"What do you mean?"

"You mean to tell me that your trifling ass can't smell that shit?" I asked.

I went to pick up my son. He was soaking wet and smelled sour from the milk on his clothes. I was so pissed that the only thing I did was grabbed his car seat and went downstairs.

"Where you taking my son?" she yelled.

"Yo, you betta be glad that I don't beat your ass. I make sure that you get enough bread every week to make sure that you live nice and you got this bitch smelling like a sewer. While you nasty bitches laughing, you be in there also and haven't said a fucking thing about this house being nasty."

I put KJ in the car and went straight to my house. As soon as we walked in the house, we went straight to the bathroom where I ran his water in his tub. I took off all his clothes, threw them in the trash, and bathed my son over and over. I took him out of the tub, took him into his room, rubbed him down in lotion and put some diaper cream on. I threw him on some clothes made him a couple bottles and we were heading over to my parents' crib.

When I arrived at my parents' house, I heard music playing from the living room, and the house was smelling right.

"MA!" I yelled.

Walking into the kitchen what I saw before me almost made me throw up and drop KJ. Pops had Moms bent over the counter, banging the hell out of her.

"OH MY GOD!!" I yelled.

My Pops looked back at me like nigga while my Moms was trying to him get to stop. The whole sight was a combination of funny and disgusting at the same time. I walked my ass back into the living room and poured me a drink because after that I damn sure needed it. I heard my mom cursing Pops out in the kitchen while he was talking about, "Shit the boy know we fucking." I swear my pops is wild.

Pops come walking out of the kitchen with a drink in his hand.

"What you doing here, lil' nigga?"

"I came to bring your grandson by." I looked with my face scrunched up.

He sat the glass down, took KJ out of his seat and sat down in his chair.

"Thank God you got our genes cause ya momma's... sheesh," Pops said.

I had to laugh because at his age, he couldn't or wouldn't care what comes out of his mouth. My mom finally appeared after thirty minutes or so looking like a lil' kid that got caught hunching in their momma house.

"When I went to go pick up KJ, you should've seen the house. It was trash, clothes, and shit everywhere and smelled like someone died in there," I told her

"Is that place in your name?" Pops asked

"Yeah, mines only," I replied.

"You know you're going to be responsible for any damage that she has done to them people place."

"I know. I'm hiring a cleaning crew to go clean the house from top to bottom, and if she can't keep it clean after that, KJ will be staying with me, and she can find somewhere else to go," I replied.

"So her trifling ass can't clean up behind herself and think that my baby about to be staying up in filth. NO ma'am KJ can stay right here until she can figure that shit out," Moms said.

"You make your appointment with the lawyer yet?"

"I have a meeting with him in a few days."

"Tell that cleaning company that you want pictures of the house before they clean it up," Moms said.

While I was sitting listening to my mom fuss about Tara, my mind wandered off to Serenity and the soft ass lips that she had.

Me: What you doing, Ma?

Serenity: Sitting at my desk wishing I was in my bed.

Me: Can I join you?

Serenity: You sure can.

Me: What you doing tonight?

Serenity: After last night, nothing at all. Shower and bed.

Me: I wanted to chill with you.

Serenity: If you want to come over here, I can cook dinner or whatever.

Me: Bet. Text me the addy.

SERENITY WAS A COOL CHICK, and I was starting to dig her. She is on top of her shit, and I like that about her. Plus, she had a kid. I sat around the house with my parents for a little while longer telling them how today's meeting with the Kash and the executives at the label went. I was going to chill longer, that was until Pops started talking about a replay of the kitchen with Mom. When he started talking like that, I had to get from around him. I was packing up KJ when Mom told me to leave him because he was already sleep and come to get him in the morning. I wasn't one of those dudes that like to drop off my seed, but I knew better than to argue with my mom.

I was going to head to the studio to bang out some tracks that I had in my head. That was something that I did on the side that only a few knew about. I was multi-talented.

When I pulled up to the studio, it was a couple cars in the parking lot that I hadn't seen before but that wasn't anything new because it was about three or four different recording studios in there. I nodded to the security guard and headed to the room that I had reserved. When I walked in, there were about five or six people already in there. I walked out of the room, looked at the room number to make sure that I wasn't in the wrong room, and walked back in.

"Can I help you, homie?" One of the guys asked.

"Yeah, I have this studio reserved and been reserved," I replied.

"Well, you need to speak with the person in charge because they gave me this room," the dude said.

While he was doing all the talking, I was already on the phone with Benji; he worked for me and my Karter.

"Yo, you need to come down here. You booked someone in my studio?" I questioned.

"I'll be right there, Mr. Sterling," Benji said.

IT TOOK Benji all of two minutes to walk into the room and explain that this was, in fact, my room and they needed to switch rooms. Of course, there was a lot of talking under their breath, but no one had the balls to direct their remarks to me, so I wasn't worried about it. As soon as they cleared out, I cleaned up all the trash and shit that they had all over. I plugged in my USB that had all the beats that I was working on.

Once I turned the music on, all the stress and drama that I had going on seemed to fade into the back of my head. I had been working for almost four hours when I realized that I hadn't eaten anything and now my stomach was on empty. I glanced down at my phone and noticed that I had some calls from Karter, Nisha, and a few text messages from Serenity. I decided to call Serenity instead of texting her back.

"Hello."

"What's good? My bad, I was in the studio working on some beats and lost track of time."

"It's fine. I was just seeing what you had a taste for dinner?" She asked.

"I'm an easy man to please as long as it tastes good, I'm straight. You decide."

"Okay. I guess I'll think of something and see you at eight," she replied.

"Bet."

I HUNG up and packed up my stuff; it was now six o'clock, and I had to go home to shower and change clothes. I lived about thirty minutes from the studio, but there wasn't any traffic, so it took me about half the time. As I was driving, I sent Nisha a text asking her to order me some flowers and I would pick them up on my way to Serenity's house.

As I pulled up in my parking lot, I jumped out and headed upstairs in the elevator. When I made it to the house, I went to start the shower, and turned on some Rod Wave. He was an artist out of Florida that I fucked with the long way. I jumped in the shower and handled my business. I didn't have to worry about a haircut because I got that last night. As I was in the shower, Tara called me, and I sent her ass to voicemail. I was going to answer her calls when I was ready and not a moment sooner. Before I could get out of the shower good, my pops called saying Tara called the house talking about she was about to call the cops on me and say I stole my son if I didn't answer her call.

After telling my pops that I wasn't answering shit, we disconnected from each other, and I finished getting ready. I threw on something simple: a white t-shirt with some grey sweatpants, some sneakers and a ball cap. I grabbed my phones and keys and headed back out of the door. I jumped into my navy blue Charger and made my way to the florist to get Serenity's roses then it was off to the address that she sent me. Karter called me again, but he would have to wait unto I leave Serenity's house to talk.

As I was heading to Serenity's house, I went ahead and called Nisha back because she was trying to get with the lawyers ASAP in reference to this custody and visitation arrangements with Tara.

"Who you ordering flowers and shit for now, boy?" she asked, laughing.

"I know you going to let me live. Nah, it's this lil' shorty that I'm feeling hard."

"As long as she isn't like ya baby momma, I'm cool."

"Oh, let me tell you about that shit. Man, I pulled up to her crib, walk into the house, and she got shit everywhere. Trash overflowing, dishes in the sink, and it smelled like a landfill."

"I told you that time I went over there they was talking about her house. They said you can smell it coming from under the door."

"The bad part is that the chicks she hangs with aren't her real friends or they would've told her to clean that nasty ass house," I stated.

"Right. I texted you because the lawyers were trying to set up an appointment to speak with you, so I just set it for Friday at two," Nisha said.

"Ight, that sounds like a plan. Make sure you set it on my calendar with a couple reminders."

I hung up from Nisha as I was pulling onto Serenity's street. It was just what I imagined from her. It was a quiet neighborhood with the kids riding up and down the street on their bikes. Much different from how Karter and I grew up, but it still gave me joy to see kids enjoying their childhood. As I pulled into the driveway, I was met by a little fella sitting on the steps tying his shoe. When I opened the door, his eyes widened like silver dollars; it was like he was shocked.

"Oh snap, it's Smoove," he yelled.

"What's up, lil' man?" I replied.

"My name is Caleb, and I already know that you are Smoove," he replied.

"Actually, my name is Kyron. My friends and family call me that so you can too."

Once he said my name, all the kids ran over to me and wanted to shake my hand. It was like clockwork that the ice cream truck came down the street.

"Y'all want some ice cream?" I asked.

"YES!" they all yelled.

I flagged down the truck and let the kids pick out what they wanted off the truck. About a hundred and fifty dollars later, all the kids had their ice cream and was thanking me and riding off on their bikes. I walked back to the car, grabbed Serenity's flowers, and headed to the door. I knocked onto the door and waited a couple more minutes, but there was no answer.

"Go head in the house, K. Mom got the music playing; she can't hear the door," Caleb yelled, riding past the house.

Following the instructions that I was given, I opened the door, and I was hit in the face with all the flavors that Serenity had going on in the kitchen.

"Serenity!" I yelled.

"I'm in the kitchen," she replied.

I walked down the hall and saw that she had pictures on a wall of her, Kash, Caleb and another chick that I hadn't seen before. I assumed that it was her other best friend that she told me about. When I turned the corner to the kitchen, Serenity was bent over doing something in the oven. When she rose up, she turned around, and this was the first time that I had seen her in a natural state. Granted she didn't wear a lot of makeup anyway, but I could tell that she didn't have any on and she was rocking a pair of Cartier eyeglasses.

"Oh shit, you scared me," she said.

"Who you thought that was calling your name?" I questioned.

"Are those for me?" she asked, pointing to the flowers that I was holding in my hand.

"Yeah," I replied, handing them to her.

"These are beautiful."

She went under the cabinet in the kitchen, pulled out a vase, and walked over to the kitchen sink.

"What you got smelling good in here?'

"I made a honey-glazed pork tenderloin with roasted potatoes and green beans," she announced.

"Well, it sounds like you know how to cook," I replied.

"Oh, I get down in these pots, don't sleep on my skills," she said.

I pulled up a stool that was at the island and continued to watch her move around the kitchen. While she was cooking, we talked about different things, like our kids. I gave her some insight on my background and how I was raised. I told her about the issues that I was having with my baby momma. She gave me some pointers on how to deal with her and make sure that I document everything that I see and take pictures. She also let it slip out that she also works with Child Protective Services. If need be, she had no problems with removing children out of bad situations if it meant that they would be better with a family member than their parent.

I knew I had to keep that in my right pocket in case I need to call on her about my situation. Caleb had come into the kitchen with ice cream all over his face.

"What is that on your face?" Serenity asked.

"Ice cream, K brought it for me," he responded.

"Who is K?"

Pointing to me, Serenity realized who he was talking about.

"Yeah, I brought him and all his friends ice cream when I pulled up," I replied.

"We will be eating in a few minutes so don't go far," she said.

I WATCHED as Serenity and her son interacted with each other. I could tell that they had a close relationship which was good because young guys needed their mothers growing up.

"Don't forget to put your basketball clothes in the washer for your game tomorrow," she yelled.

"Oh, lil' dude balls?" I asked.

"Yes, he plays at the Boys and Girls Club over in Oakhurst," she announced.

"Oh word? That's one of the spots that Kash has on my list to go visit," I replied.

"You want some water or something to drink?" she asked.

"I'll take a glass of water," I replied.

WE WALKED into the living room where she turned on the TV and passed me the remote. I scrolled through the TV trying to find something to watch.

"You can get comfortable," she replied.

I found a show on TV One to watch, put the remote and my

phones on the table and sat back to chill while she finished with dinner.

Kashmir

I have been replaying last night in my head over and over again. What in the hell was I thinking to allow myself to be carefree and maybe have ruined a perfectly good working relationship with Karter? Yes, he is the definition of fine, and yes, he is every definition of a real man. I was currently taking a run in my neighborhood to shake these thoughts and try to ease some of the stress that I had. I was just about to my house when I noticed a car in the driveway which I didn't recognize because mine was in the garage. As I got closer, I realized that it was Karter leaning against his car, scrolling through his phone.

I wonder if I run past the house, will he notice me?

Deciding to put on my big girl panties, I walked up the driveway and stood in front of him.

"So you're just going to sneak out of the room and hotel without saying anything?" he asked.

"I felt that it was better that way. It was something that we both wanted, so there was no need to make it into something that it isn't," I replied.

"What do you mean, make it to something that it isn't?" he questioned.

"Look, you're a married man, and I'm newly out of a relationship. We both know that this was rebound sex so let's not play the games."

"Woah, slow down. Let's go inside; we don't need everyone in our business," he replied.

WHEN WE GOT into the house, I went to the kitchen to wash my hands and grab me something to drink. Karter, on the other hand, grabbed a seat on the barstool at the island.

"So what is all this rebound stuff you talking about? I'm a very picky man when it comes to who I fuck. I don't sleep with every chick that I come in contact with, so you can slow all that shit down from here."

"I just figured-"

"Figured what? That because I got money, nice ass car, and got swag for days that I'll sleep with anyone that will throw their pussy at me?" he cut me off.

Well, he just shut me all the way up. I was standing there speechless because he looked fine as hell when he was mad.

"So what are we doing then?" I asked.

"We are being grown and handling things as they come," he replied, walking up on me.

He backed me up into the refrigerator and just stood there staring at me.

"Do you think that you can handle, us working together and maybe more? Because I'm not going anywhere."

Lord, this man here had me hot and bothered, and if it wasn't for the fact that I was sweaty, I probably would've started something right there in the kitchen.

"You looking at me like you like what you see. Let's go to the bathroom so that you can take a shower."

He didn't have to tell me twice. I kicked off my shoes at the bottom of the steps and headed up, he followed me taking his off and proceeded to come up. Before we made it up to the top of the steps, his phone was ringing, and he was answering it.

"Yeah,"

I watched as he kept coming up the stairs, and once we made it to the door, he stopped and listened to what the person on the line was saying.

"I'll be right there," he spoke and hung up.

I guess he must have seen the disappointment on my face because he walked over to me and kissed me on the forehead.

"I got to make a couple moves, some shit popped off that I gotta go handle," he said.

"Ok," I replied.

"I'll try to make it back once I finish, but I'll text you either way," he said.

He ran down the stairs in a hurry and out of the door. He was peeling rubber out of the driveway. I went into the bathroom to start my shower and decided to call my girls on three way to see what they were up to.

"Hello," Starr said with an attitude.

"Eww, who pissed in your cereal?" I asked.

"My bad, girl. Shyne just got a call and had to leave right when I was about to get some dick," she said.

"Well, TMI, and wait. Shyne? When did this happen?" I asked.

"Chile, we been kicking it ever since we ran into his ass at that time at the club," she replied

"Hold on, I'm responding to Serenity. She talking about she got company and will call us back."

"Who she got over there?" Starr asked,

"Probably Kyron ass," I replied.

"Back that shit up. What her and Kyron got going on?" Starr asked.

"They went on a date and all, chile. We got a lot of catching up to do," I replied.

"I see. What's new with you?"

"Nothing much just working and maintaining," I replied.

"I feel you. So have you seen what that fine ass man dick look like?" she said, laughing.

"Well..."

"Bitch, you didn't! Was it good?"

"Girl, I can't even explain to you the feeling," I replied.

"You little dirty whore," she laughed.

"We gotta do dinner or something. Let's meet up since I don't have nothing to do."

"Yeah, give me like thirty minutes. Outback?" she asked.

"That will work," I replied and disconnected the call.

. . .

I JUMPED into the shower and lathered my body. I need to make myself an appointment to get my nails, and hair done. I threw on a cute lil' dress with some sandals and headed out of the door. By the time that I was pulling into the restaurant parking lot, Starr was getting out of her car. We greeted each other and headed into the door to get a table. There was about a fifteen-minute wait, so we decided that we were going to go to the bar to have a couple drinks.

"So tell me what's going on with you and ole boy," Starr said as she sipped her drink.

"Girl, it's so much," I replied and began telling her everything that happened.

AS WE WERE SEATED, I continued to tell her how things started and how we came to this point. Once I was finished, she sat there with her mouth wide open. She went on to tell me how her and my cousin have been spending time getting to know each other, although she has known him since we were little. I guess even though you know someone in passing, you never really get to know them. Shyne always had a crush on Starr, but she would always play him to the left.

We ordered, and while we were waiting on our food, Starr must've gotten a text from Shyne because she was smiling from ear to ear. It felt good to just hang out with her for a little bit. We both were so busy during the days that we barely checked in on each other. While we were eating our food, a group of women kept staring in our direction. I couldn't make out the face because I hadn't seen any of them before.

"Star, do you see them chicks over there?" I nodded in their direction.

"Yeah, what about them?" She questioned.

"Do you know any of them?" I asked.

"Come on now, you know I do not hang with chicks other than my besties," she replied.

Taking another sip of my drink, it finally clicked where I saw one of the chicks before.

"Girl, now that I think about it, that is Karter's soon-to-be ex over there," I said.

"Girl, I know you lying."

I was so busy texting Karter about his ex that I didn't even notice that they were heading my way.

"Excuse me, you the bitch that's fucking my husband?" she asked.

Looking up from my phone, I stared at the woman that stood before me. She was a nice-looking woman, but she and I were on two different levels. Taking another sip of my drink, I gathered my composure and thought about what my response would be to her.

"If you want to know if I was fucking your husband, I would think that you need to be asking him that. Furthermore, what your ex-husband and I have going on should be none of your concern. If I were you, I would move around instead to trying to flaunt something that doesn't even mean anything to me," I replied.

"Look, just stay away from my husband," she replied.

"And if I choose not to, what are you going to do?" I smirked.

"Oh, you don't want to see what I will do."

Raising out of my seat because threats wasn't something that I took kindly, Starr was standing up out of hers also. Before I would say another word, a voice boomed behind me that scared the shit out of me.

"We got a problem here?" the voice said.

"No, baby. I was telling your friend that she needed to leave you alone and let us work things out."

"Bailee, there isn't shit to work out. Now I don't know why you fronting for your friends, but that ship has sailed," he stated, grabbing my waist.

"Starr, your ass out here about to fight?" Shyne asked.

"If one of these bitches touched my friend, I would," she replied.

"Oh, I know that you didn't just walk past me like you ain't see me here?" some other chick said.

"Oh, it's no pressure over here. Shyne, go ahead and speak to ya people," Starr said.

"Yeah, that's what I thought," she replied.

"Bitch, I will beat the brakes off your ass. Don't let the cute face fool you, I will fuck your short ass up," Starr replied.

They were off from there going back and forth exchanging words while the others added their two cents in.

WHILE KARTER WAS GOING BACK and forth with his wife and Shyne was arguing with Star and the other chick, I took the opportunity to pay my bill and walk right the hell out leaving them there. This was exactly what I didn't want or need right now, no fucking drama. I got in my car and sat there for a moment laughing to myself thinking how crazy that entire scene was. I started my car and headed home; I needed a glass of wine and a blunt ASAP. As I was driving home, Starr called me. I ignored her call. Karter called me and I did the same with him. I was embarrassed at the fact that they both stood there and made a scene in a restaurant.

I pulled my car into the garage, immediately took off my shoes, and ran upstairs to change clothes. I threw on a short dress, wrapped my hair up, and came back downstairs to pour me a glass of wine, sit on my back porch and listen to music. Hell, it was a warm enough night that I might just take a dip in my pool. Before I could even relax, my door was opening, and Starr ass was yelling my name.

Damn.

I just sat there hoping that she would get the picture and leave, but her ass came right outside with Karter and Shyne right behind her.

"What the fuck all of y'all doing here?" I asked.

"Why the hell you leave?" Karter asked.

"Look, I'm not about to sit there and watch you argue with your wife. If y'all want to work it out, by all means, go ahead but leave me the fuck out of it," I replied.

"Hold up, shorty. Who are you cursing at?" he questioned.

"You. All you niggas are the same. Selfish as fuck and only think about yourselves."

"Woah. First off, don't ever compare me to any of the niggas that you been with because I damn sure ain't them. Now, I apologize if you felt slighted because I was making shit crystal clear with my ex. Me selfish? Sweetheart, you haven't even stepped into my world, but I promise you selfish isn't in my vocabulary," he replied.

"Well, this shit sound like a lover's fight," Shyne said, trying to be funny.

"Shyne, getcho ass out my damn house trying to make jokes and shit," I replied.

"It's a nice night out; I'm about to go put my bathing suit on," Starr said.

"No, you're not. You're about to leave with Shyne and Karter's ass."

She paid me no mind while she went upstairs and Shyne was now in my kitchen making him something to eat. I swear they get on my nerves. Deciding that I was going to join Starr, I went upstairs and put my bathing suit on. As I was coming back down the hall, I could hear Starr and Shyne in the guestroom laughing.

"Aye, don't be trying to get you none in my damn house, Shyne," I giggled through the door.

"Mind ya business, cuz," Shyne replied.

WHEN I MADE IT DOWNSTAIRS, Karter was now sitting in the chair, listening to the music while doing something with a cup beside him.

"Comfortable much?" I asked.

"Shorty, kill the attitude," he replied.

I didn't say another word to him. I grabbed my cup and blunt, sat it on the edge of the pool and jumped in. I could believe that I just had a full argument with a man that I'm not even in a relationship with. What in the hell was really going on?

13

Karter

I sat there and watched Kash pouting in the pool. I wasn't sure what she was even mad about it wasn't like we had any labels or anything like that. I wanted to say something to her, but I figured that it would only make matters worse, so I sat back and sipped my drink. I had a lot on my mind anyway. One of my trucks that had my new shipment in it was hit, and I lost a grip on that. Then I had to deal with shit with Bailee. I wasn't sure what she thought was going to happen but approaching Kash about something that she didn't have anything to do with wasn't the right way to handle it.

"Kash," I called.

"Yeah?"

"You want to talk about what just happened a couple minutes ago," I asked.

"We can if you want," she replied.

PULLING my shirt over my head and taking my pants off to reveal the shorts that I had underneath, I got into the pool with my drink.

"What was all that about?" I asked.

"I guess I had a flashback from the shit that I used to go through with my ex. The countless women that would approach us whenever we were together, the disrespect; I just had a moment," she said.

"Sweetheart, it was never my intention to disrespect you, I respect you to the fullest. I was trying to diffuse the situation that was going on because I know how things can go when it comes to Bailee. She real hood and ghetto and doesn't think when she is mad, so I wanted to make sure that you were safe. If that looked like it was pushing you to the side, then I'm sorry."

"What are we doing, Karter?" I asked.

"What you mean?"

"This right here, last night, everything."

"Well, right now, we are in this pool enjoying the water and having a conversation. Last night, what I thought was two adults elevating some sexual tension that has been between us since the day that we met. We don't have to put labels on exactly what we are doing but just know that I do see myself with you in the long run."

"So you see a future with me?" she questioned.

"Most definitely. You're smart, driven, about your business, and sexy as fuck."

"I just don't want you to think that this is how I do with all of my clients," she replied.

"For one, I'm not the client; my brother is. So what you and I have going on shouldn't affect any of his business. When we're working, we're working and when we not, we not."

I walked closer to her because she was looking good as hell in that bathing suit that she was wearing. I wanted to rip it off of her and fuck her right in the pool, but I had to remember that Shyne and Starr was here.

"You know once they leave, this is coming off, right?" I asked.

She shook her head yes, and I kissed her deeply when Starr and Shyne walked out.

"Well, it looks like they have made up," Starr said.

"Yeah and y'all did too," Kash said, laughing.

. . .

STARR AND SHYNE jumped in the pool, we drank and listened to the music. They smoked, I watched. It was about one o'clock when Shyne and Starr decided they were ready to leave. Kash cleaned up the house and then showered. I was handling some business while she was doing that and went to take mines. By the time that I finished showering, she was already sleep. It was cool though I was going to get her in the morning. I turned on Netflix and fell asleep with the TV watching me. I was awakened by Kash riding the fuck out of me. I don't know when she got up there, but she was sweaty as hell like she had been working out.

"Well, good morning!" I said.

"Mmmmmm. Good morning," she moaned.

Flipping her over, I began to pound her insides while she begged me to go deeper. I guess the saying was true; the quiet ones were freaks.

"This is what you want?" I asked.

"Yes, right there," she replied.

"Get on them knees," I said, slapping her ass.

Good Lawd, she had the perfect arch in the back that made my dick harder than it was before.

"Shit girl, hold on," I said.

"Oh my god," she said.

I gave her long, deep strokes. Like I was trying to make her feel it in her stomach. She was still tight as shit, so I knew that this was some Grade-A pussy. I was trying to hold back the urge to cum, but she once again started throwing it back.

"Go ahead and cum; I'm right behind you."

"Shit! Shit! Shit!" she said. The next thing I knew she was squirting,

"Oh, I see you a squirted, huh!" I said.

As she continued to squirt, I unload everything that was in my sack inside of her. I fell on the side of her trying to catch my breath.

"I don't know what was wrong with that nigga to be messing around on you, but I want to thank him," I said.

"You so crazy, get up. You want breakfast?" she asked, walking to the bathroom.

"Yeah, I can eat. You going into the office today?" I asked.

"No, I'm working from home. I have to work on my business plan for opening my own PR firm," she replied.

"Oh word, you're going to step out on your own?"

"Yeah, I'm getting tired of having to answer to someone else about how I work with my clients," she replied.

She started the water in the shower and stepped in. I scrolled through my phone when I received a message of a video from one of my neighbor's camera showing somebody going up to my house and breaking a window. The next thing that it showed was smoke coming out of the window and the person running off. I sent the video to my computer tech, Beanz so that he could enhance the image and try to match the face. Once I finished with that, I received a text from my dude at the club telling me how Bailee came through last night. I'm guessing after the fight and showed her ass at the club, dancing on niggas and starting fights. I swear at what age was she going to stop.

Nick texted me that one of the houses had sold above what the asking price was because the furniture was included. I told him to let me know before pops came and signed the papers so that I could go by and take any personal things out of the house of the kids and I. He also told me that the house that I was looking that the owner accepted my all-cash offer and would be ready to sign the papers by the end of the week.

It was a good feeling to be starting fresh without all the drama that was following behind me, mainly Bailee. Speaking of that, I texted my lawyer that I wanted full custody of the girls. I didn't think that she was able to raise the girls and still live the lifestyle that she wanted. And the text that I had received this morning confirmed what I had been feeling.

14

Kyron

I woke up this morning sleeping beside Serenity, but I still had the clothes from last night. I don't even remember coming to the bedroom. Last I remember we were watching a movie on the couch after we ate.

"Caleb, get your butt off that damn game and get dressed," Serenity yelled.

She walked back into her room with a glass of juice in her hand wearing a robe and her hair tied up.

"Well, good morning," she said.

"Morning," I replied, standing up to stretch.

"Did you sleep well?"

"Hell yeah, I don't even remember coming up here," I replied.

"Well, I'm getting ready to get Caleb off to school," she replied.

Caleb came walking into the room with his school clothes on and walked into Serenity's bathroom.

"Caleb, what I told you about walking into my room?"

"Ma, I needed my brush. Hey, K," he said.

"What's up, man?"

"I gotta go make a couple moves and go check on my son," I said, grabbing my phone.

I went downstairs as Serenity followed behind me and went into the kitchen. I walked over to her and kissed her. Being with Serenity gave me a sense of peace, something that I haven't felt with a chick in a long time.

"Last night was cool, the next time I'll cook," I said.

"You cook?" she asked.

"Yeah, I can do a little something," I replied.

Serenity walked me to the door and stood there as I got into my car. I checked messages, and of course, there were messages from Tara threating me if I didn't bring KJ back home. I had a message from my lawyer that he had the paperwork drawn up for our arrangement and that he was sending it out today. I started my car and headed to my parents' house before I headed home.

When I pulled up to the house, I sat in the car for a couple moments reflecting on my evening with Serenity. The evening just flowed, we laughed, talked about movies and even went back and forth about football.

I went into the house to find that my son was in there raising hell about something sitting in his chair while my mom's cooked breakfast.

"Aye, what's going on in here?" I asked.

"Nothing, just KJ fussing because nobody is picking his spoiled tail up," Mom replied.

"How was he last night?" I asked.

"It was nothing that I couldn't handle," she replied.

"How was your night?"

"It was cool. I had a lil' date if that is what you want to call it," I replied.

"A what? O, please fill me in on this lucky lady."

"She's cool; I met her on my way coming over here the other day. She is actually best friends with Kash, my PR person."

"Oh, your father told me about her. He says that she does not play with you."

"Yeah, she's hard on me, but that's what I need. She has me doing a total image revamp and all,"

"Well, that's good then. You need it especially with your brother working with you," My pops said, entering the room.

"So what is going on with that girl Tara?" pops asked.

"I guess we will see in a couple hours. My lawyer is having the custody and support papers delivered today," I replied.

I took KJ and went upstairs to change him and put on some clothes while my mom finished cooking breakfast. I called Karter to see what he was up to since I hadn't talked to him when he called me.

"AYO!" I said.

"What's up?" he replied.

"Shid, just calling you back I was working then I went over to ole girl house."

"I see you making moves; I peeped your IG."

"I'm at our folk's house. I thought you would be here this morning getting this good breakfast that moms is cooking with ya greedy ass."

"Nah, Kash cooking right now."

"Nigga, come again?"

"You a fool but, yeah we chilling if that is what you want to call it," he responded.

"Now, you know I know better than that. There is no such thing as chilling in your book."

"Nah, it's nothing like that, we just vibing and chilling," he replied.

"Aye, let me talk to her real quick since she there," I said.

I HEARD him yelling her name, and she got onto the phone.

"Hello."

"Kash, I need you to hook me up with the Boys and Girls club by Serenity's house. I told Serenity that you did already."

"You told my bestie what?" she questioned.

"That I was going to be volunteering there. I was trying to make a good impression," I said.

"Don't start with the lies to her. I'll see what I can do though," she replied, handing the phone back to Karter.

"Yeah, what you got planned today?" I asked.

"I'm signing the papers to my new crib in a couple hours and meeting with Pops about a couple things. What's up?" he asked.

"Nothing, just came to get KJ before I head home."

We talk a couple minutes more then I headed back downstairs to get something to eat that mom was cooking. She made me a plate while I packed KJ's things, and we headed out of the house.

By the time that I had made it home, Tara ass had started blowing up my phone once again. I guess she must've realized that KJ wasn't still there after she sobered up.

"What, man?" I yelled.

"When you bringing my baby home and you think you funny serving me with these damn papers?"

"Ain't nothing funny about anything when it comes to my son. Look, did the cleaning crew come over there?" I asked.

I knew the answer because they had sent the invoice and pictures that I wanted.

"Yeah, they came and cleaned up with masks and protective suits and shit on," She replied.

"I'm not about to have my baby over in that filth so until I see that you can keep that house clean with no help, KJ will be with me," I replied.

"So I guess that I'll just call the cops then," she threatened.

"Do what you gotta do," I replied and hung up.

Tara thought she had the one up on me thinking that if she called the cops, I would bitch up and take my son back. I got KJ settled in his room and texted my lawyer and let him know what just happened with Tara and her threats. I also forwarded over the pictures that the cleaning crew sent to add to my file. I wasn't no dumb nigga, I may act a fool at times, but I was smart as hell.

I went into the kitchen to warm up the plate that my moms had made me and sat down to eat while I texted Serenity.

Me: I had a nice time last night.

Serenity: I did too. What you up to?

Me: Just finished getting with my lawyer on this custody case.

Serenity: I see. I just made it in the office. Looks like I will be in the field today working on a case.

Me: 'Ight. Let me know if you get close to me, I can order lunch and meet you somewhere.

Serenity Sounds like a plan.

15

Karter

WHEN I FINISHED the call with my brother, I went back upstairs to lay in Kash's bed until she finished with breakfast. I wasn't sure what it was about her, but I was comfortable as hell. When I was out doing dirt, I would never stay long enough to catch my breath. I would finish fucking the chick, shower then I would bounce. Kash was different; she had goals and dreams that she wanted to accomplish. Not just getting with a nigga that had money, she wanted to make her own money.

"KARTER," Kash yelled.

"Ight," I responded.

I threw on my shorts, grabbed my phones, and headed back downstairs to where Kash had cooked so much you would think that other people were coming over.

"Girl, what you cooked all this food for?" I asked.

"I wasn't sure what you wanted, so I cooked a little of everything," she replied.

She made me a plate putting everything that she made and

poured me a glass of orange juice before she sat down and made her own plate. I was starving, and I didn't even realize it. I looked down at my plate, and everything that Kash put on there was gone.

"Well damn, what did you do open your mouth and scrap the food in?" she laughed.

"A nigga was hungry I guess," I replied.

I sat there and sent Shyne a text that I needed to get with him ASAP to see if he found out who hit my shipment. I received a couple text from the girls this morning, but it was too late to respond to them because they were already in class. I made a mental note to call them when they got out to see what was going on.

"What you got planned today?" I asked Kash.

"I'm doing a little work today, nothing major," she replied.

"Ight. I'm about to bounce because I got a couple things I need to check on, got to go sign these papers for the sale of my old house and the purchase of the new one all in the same day."

"Oh, congrats on both of those," she replied.

She got up from the table and began cleaning the table and kitchen.

"You want me to help you?' I asked.

"No, you're good. Go ahead and start your day," she said over her shoulder.

I went upstairs, put my shirt on, and headed back downstairs.

"Let's do lunch today. Say about two?" I asked, grabbing her by the waist.

"That sounds nice," she replied as she kissed my lips.

I left out of her house and headed to the hotel so that I could change clothes and head over to Nick's office to sign what I needed with Pops and go on about my business. By the time that I had made it to the hotel, Bailee was blowing up my phones with calls and texts asking me to call her ASAP. I wasn't in the mood to deal with her bullshit right now, so I would get back to her when I decided to call her. I went into my room, grabbed me something to wear, and headed to the shower.

When I finished, I got dressed and headed back out the door to go to my meeting that I was now late for. I sent Nick and my pops a text to let them know that I was on my way and would be there in fifteen minutes. I received a call from my tech dude, Beanz that was working on the image that I had sent him of the guy that started the fire at my house.

"Yeah," I said into the Bluetooth.

"So I did a search and got a hit on the face from your house, but you are not going to like this," he said.

"Don't say nothing. I'll be over that way in an hour," I replied and hung up.

I never discussed business on the phone; my pops taught me that a long time ago. I pulled up to Nick's office and Pops was outside smoking a blunt. I swear he thinks he is the coolest man alive and you betta not tell him different.

"What's up, old man?"

"The sky. Nigga, you're late," he replied.

"My bad, I wasn't at the hotel this morning," I replied.

"Well, come on so I can get back to your mother. I told her I would take her to get this new damn car she wanted," he stated.

"Oh, what you buying her?' I asked.

"She wants that Cadillac XT5 or some shit like that. You know she gotta be different and want something no one else has," he replied.

We waited in the conference room while Nick was on the phone, I texted Kash to see what she was doing, but Nick walked in before she had a chance to respond.

"Gentlemen, are we ready to do this?"

"You damn right," Pop said.

"So Karter, this is the paperwork for the house you wanted, all-cash offer and they have thirty days to turn the property over to you."

"Pops, I need you to sign here and here for the sale of the house. This is the amount that will be deposited into your account that the rest will be deposited into the other account," he said to us cutting give us both eye.

Both Pops and I signed our name on the dotted line. Then Pops got up first to leave while I stayed back and talked a little with Nick about the other houses on the market. He told me that he even had a buyer for the house that had the fire, but I wanted to make sure that everything was right before I sold it off. We talked a couple minutes more, and then I headed out to Shane's house.

Shane's house was like Fort Knox with security camera's everywhere. You would think he was a spy or something the way he had it locked down. When I walked in, he was sitting in his living room on the couch.

"What's up?" I said.

"Yeah, like I was saying you're not going to like this." He explained as I followed him down the hall to his office. When I walked in, he had about ten to fifteen computer screens mounted to the wall. He began to start the video and paused and zoomed in on the face as he entered my house.

"You know him?" Shane asked.

"Nah, I can't say that I do."

"Well, you should since he is your wife's first cousin."

"What the fuck you talking about?" I questioned.

"Yeah, it's her cousin," he replied, pulling up some pictures of Bailee and him with her mother and aunt from Facebook.

"You mean to tell me that this broad sent this nigga to burn down my house?"

"That's what it looks like my dude."

As he was talking, I zoned out and went to sending texts to my hitman, letting them know that I needed them ASAP. I was now done playing with Bailee and anyone else that was in my way.

"Send me all the information that you have," I said, walking out the office.

By the time that I reached the front door, my phone was going off with the information that Shane had prepared. As I headed to the warehouse, I wanted to make a detour and choke the shit out of Bailee for her stupid ass idea, but now she was getting ready to be wearing all black because of her choice.

I pulled up to the warehouse, and all my captains were already there. I walked inside, and everyone stood up like they always did.

"Be seated," I said.

"So, we are here trying to figure out how and why the shipment from yesterday didn't make it back. Who wants to start?" Shyne said.

No one said anything. They looked at each other to see who was going to speak first.

"Where is the driver?" I asked.

A middle-age guy stood up and raised his hand.

"What's your name?" I asked."

"Stan," the man replied.

"Stan, so tell me what happened," I stated.

"I was taking our normal routine and the next thing I know two black SUV's pull behind me. I kept on driving and then two more jumped in front of me and slammed on their brakes, causing me to stop. Before I had a chance to grab my gun, a dude was standing at my window with a mask on, and a gun pointed at my head," Stan replied.

"So do you think that it was a setup?" Shyne asked.

"Yes, because they knew exactly where to go look for the product in the truck," Stan said.

"Ight, you can sit down," I said.

"So we will be changing shit up because someone is leaking information in one of y'all crews. Once I find out who it is though, it will be hell to pay. Tell people to get the black ready, I don't like taking losses and I damn sure don't like losing money," I said.

"Y'all can go," Shyne said.

As everyone cleared out, I walked to my office to meet with my hitters Black and Slim I met them years ago when I had an issue with a Cuban that thought he was going to take over my streets. We have been tight ever since.

"So here is the information on who I want y'all to find. This my soon-to-be ex's people so ain't no telling where he is now."

"So are we killing him or bringing him back to you?" Slim asked.

"For now bring him back, once I get what I need then y'all can do what y'all do. I already sent the payment to the offshore account so it should be there in a couple hours," I said.

"'Ight. Well, let's get to work." Black stood and we shook hands.

"You got everything under control here?" I asked Shyne.

"Yeah, I'm straight. The other shipments came in with no problem, so I got the workers coming in to break it down for distributing," he replied.

"Hit me up if you need me," I said, walking towards the door.

When I got back into my car, I went to call Kash to see what she was up to. It was now about two, so I was hungry.

"Hey you," she said.

"What you doing?" I asked.

"Sitting at this computer screen. You took care of what you needed to do?"

"Yeah, I just finished up. You ready for lunch?" I asked.

"I have to put some clothes on, where am I meeting you?" she asked.

"I'll be there in fifteen minutes," I replied as I made a U-turn.

BY THE TIME that I made it to her house, she was checking her mailbox. I pulled in the driveway and got out to open her door. I kissed her on the lips as she got in the car. As we pulled off, Kash stuffed her mail in her purse and put it in the back.

"So where are we heading?" she asked.

Before I could respond to her, my phone rang and I connected it to my Bluetooth.

"Hello."

"Hello, Mr. Sterling. This is Principal Mills here at the girl's school. We are calling because we need you to come in to speak with us. It's very important," she said.

I sensed the urgency in her voice, so I bussed another U-turn and headed that way.

"I will be there in twenty minutes. Have you contacted their mother?" I asked.

"No sir," she replied.

"Ok, I'll be there."

"Do you want to cancel our lunch?" Kash asked.

"Nah, we already on the way to the girl's school. You can come along," I replied.

WHEN I PULLED up to the girl's school, there were police cars in the parking lot, which didn't mean anything because it could have been the resource officer. Kash stayed in the car while I went in to see what the hell was going on. I walked into the office, and the girls were sitting with Kash friend. I couldn't remember her name to save my life, so I just nodded.

"Mr. Sterling," the principal called out.

"Yes."

"Please come in," she said.

"Okay girls, I want you to stay right here. If you need anything, Mr. Greene right here will help you," she said.

I WALKED INTO THE OFFICE, and Kash friend followed behind me and closed the door.

"Hello, Mr. Sterling. My name is Serenity Hollis, and I'm with Child Protective Services. It has been brought to our attention that the girls have been coming to school with bruises on their arms, and lower back," she said, placing photos in front of me.

When she said that all I could see was red. I know they weren't sitting here telling me that Bailee's ass has been abusing my kids.

"Mr. Sterling, are you ok?" Mrs. Mills asked.

"Yes, I'm fine. So what is going to happen now?" I asked.

"The girls informed me that you and your wife have separated, which is a good thing because had you been still living in the home, I would have no choice but to file charges against you also and place the children with a relative or even in foster care. Instead, I will be releasing them to you with an understanding that the children are to have no contact with their mother until we go before the judge. I will also have to come and do a home study and make sure that the girls are in a safe environment sometime this tomorrow," she stated.

"Of course. Anything you need to do to make sure that I keep my girls I'm okay with," I replied.

"Okay, you can take the girls home," Mrs. Mills said.

I stood up and walked out of the office damn near tears at the sight of my daughters. They rushed me, causing me to stumble, but I regained my balance.

"Come on," I said, walking out of the office with murder on my mind.

When I made it back to the car, Kash was on her phone talking to someone. When she saw me and the girls, she ended the call quickly.

"Is everything okay?" she asked.

"Girls, this is Ms. Kash. Kash, this is London and Paris," I said.

"Hello," they all said at the same time.

"Y'all hungry?" I asked the girls.

"Yes," they both replied.

"Karter, you can take me to the house if you want. I will understand," Kash said.

"Girls, y'all want seafood?" I asked, ignoring her.

Kash didn't know it, but she was giving me a sense of peace that I needed right now because the hell I was about to cause was about to be shameless. I drove us to the girl's favorite seafood restaurant out on the beach. When I parked the car, the girls went into their bags and grabbed their practice shorts and shirt to get comfortable. While they were in the bathroom changing, I got us a table and took a moment to explain what was going on.

"My ex has been abusing the girls, and right now, I have custody of them until we go to court. Your friend was in there working the case," I said.

"OH NO! Wait, my friend Serenity?" she asked.

"Yeah, that's her," I replied.

The girls came out of the bathroom and asked for the keys to the car to put their clothes inside. While they went to the car, I went to the bathroom, and Kash waited for our table. When I came out, they were seated and engrossed in a full conversation.

"I was just asking the girls what is good here."

"We told her everything," Paris laughed.

"Yeah, we always order a little of everything when we come and end up taking food home," I said.

"Well I guess we will have to do that then," Kash said.

ONCE WE PLACED OUR ORDER, I watched as Kash interacted with the girls. She was laughing and joking with them and that made me glad that I decided to not take her home once I left the school. While the girls were talking, I noticed that they would take turns looking down at their phones.

"Is that ya moms calling?' I asked.

They both shook their head yes. Holding my hand out, both of them placed their phone in my hand, and I powered them off. I excused myself from the table and went outside to call Bailee.

"Yeah," she said with an attitude.

"Yo, stop calling the fucking girls before I change their number on your ass. I can't believe that you had the nerve to put your fucking hands on my babies like that. Have you lost your mind?"

"It wasn't even that bad and had they not came slick out of their mouth, I wouldn't have popped them."

"You do know that I saw the pictures from multiple occasions, right? So you can stop acting like it was only one time. Check this out, don't look for them no time soon because they aren't coming home."

"If you don't bring my kids home, I will call the cops on your ass," she replied.

"Well, I guess you gotta do what you gotta do then."

I hung up from her and walked back into the restaurant with Kash and the girls. I paid for our food, and we headed back to the city. I wanted to show the girls and Kash my new house; I knew that they would be excited. I stopped at the mall to take the girls shopping because they didn't have anything to wear and they had school in the morning.

Kash helped the girls pick out a couple things to get them through the rest of the week until I could get their things that they wanted moved for the time being. As they were shopping, Kash walked over to me to talk.

"You know you can't take them to the hotel, right?"

"Yeah, I know. I was thinking of taking them to the lake house, but that is an hour drive. So I think that I will just have them stay with my parents until I get the keys to the new house I'm going to show y'all later," I said.

"Oh, you brought a house?" she asked.

"Yeah, I closed on it today. That was one of the appointments that I had."

"Well, if you want, y'all can stay with me," she replied.

"Nah, I'm going to go over to my parents. I don't want the girls to get the wrong idea."

AFTER WE WENT SHOPPING, I took them by the new house and of course the girls loved it, even though they were just looking through the windows they tried to pick out their rooms and all. Once we finished at the house, I went ahead and dropped Kash off telling her that I would try to make it back over. As I headed over to my parents, the girls asked my fifty-eleven questions about Kash. Some I could answer and some I didn't know how to respond. As I pulled up to the house, Paris and London jumped out the car and ran inside. They had their own rooms in the house along with Kyron and I.

As I walked towards the house, my mother was standing at the door with her hands on her hips.

"Y'all staying over?" she asked.

"Yeah, I gotta talk to you and Pops about something," I replied.

I ran upstairs to check on the girls to make sure that they had started their homework and to take their showers. I went back downstairs and asked my parents to meet me in my pops' office.

"So what's going on, son?" My pops asked.

"Well, I got a call to come to Paris and London's school today. When I get there, the police and CPS was there. Come to find out that Bailee has been abusing the fucking girls, man. They had all kinds of photos of the girls' backs, faces and arms. I swear to god I want to kill Bailee's ass."

As I paced back and forth venting, I watch my mother's expression go from calm to rage and back to calm. It was almost scary watching the calmness on her face. As I waited for her to respond, my father was the first to say something.

"Well, I'm glad they had the sense enough to call you and not try to send them to a foster home or something like that," he said.

My mother still hadn't said anything yet, and I was beginning to worry. I explained to them that I would need to stay with them for a couple weeks until I moved into the house and give them the rundown on CPS doing the home visit to make sure that they were safe.

When I finished talking, my mom got up out of her chair and walked over to the safe that my father had hidden behind a picture. She put the code in to unlock and pulled out her gun.

"Ma, what are you about to do?" I asked.

"I'm about to go and have a talk with Ms. Bailee since she wants to lay hands on people," she replied.

"Ma, as much as I want to go touch her, we gotta think about the girls but trust me I got something for her. It's some other shit that I got going on with her included in it," I said.

"You better get her before I do," my mother said.

16

Kashmir

ONCE KARTER DROPPED ME OFF, I had to sit down and think about everything that happened throughout the day. I was completely shocked when we went to the girl's school only for him to come out with both of them. They were beautiful and well-mannered young ladies, but they had two different styles which was usual with sisters. Going up to my bathroom to run me a tub of water, I received a call from Serenity.

"Hey, girl," she said.

"Hey, boo. I got a bone to pick with you," I said.

"Before you start, you know damn well that if I had a chance to tell you, I would've given you the heads up."

"I know. I was just fucking with you," I replied.

"Girl, you should see the pictures of the girls. I wanted to kick her ass myself."

"I know that Karter was pissed as hell, girl."

"I know I could see it all over his face when I was talking to him. It was like he zoned out, damn near scared me."

"So anyway, what is new with you?" I asked, turning the water off.

"I had Kyron come over last night to chill."

"Bihhh, you gave him some," I said, hooking my phone to the Bluetooth.

"No girl. We just watched movies, ate dinner and chilled."

"Now I get why he wanted to volunteer at the Boys and Girls club by your house."

"Aye, he told Caleb he was. Girl, they just clicked, talking about basketball and the PlayStation."

"Aww, that is sweet. He is a good guy; he's just a hothead at times. Especially with his dumb ass baby momma," I said.

"You heard from Starr?" I asked.

"Yeah, I was with her the other day. We went for drinks and had a run-in with Karter's wife and some chick that Shyne was messing with."

"Wait, Starr messing with Shyne?"

"Girl, yeah. Her sneaky ass been messing with him since the night we seen him in the club."

"Oh, wait 'til I see her bald-headed ass. So how is everything going with Karter?"

"He is really cool people, the dick is amazing, and he treats me good," I replied.

"Bitch, you gave him some? Where the fuck have I been, under a rock or something?" she asked.

"It wasn't planned. I was tipsy the night we went out last, and I kinda slipped on his dick, no big deal," I said.

"Girl, let me go get your godson from out this building. I will talk to you later."

"Ight. Give my baby a kiss for me," I said and hung up.

I SAT in the tub for I don't know how long. I had the music going and my wine, I was just relaxing thinking of all the plans for my business. The only thing that I needed to make my dream come true was an investor. Hell, even a silent partner would do with some money.

When I finally got out of the tub, I jumped into the shower to wash off and put my favorite pajamas on. I turned on the TV and began working on some of the contracts for the clients that I had been neglecting the last couple weeks because of all the drama with Kyron and my own personal life.

I took my time and worked on one client at a time while still sipping my wine. I checked my phone to see a number kept calling my phone over and over again. I answered the phone only to be disappointed by the person that was on the other line.

"What up, baby?" Gio's dumbass said.

"What do you want?" I asked.

"I see that you moved on already. That was quick,"

"What are you talking about?" I asked, acting clueless.

"The dude from the club, that's your new nigga?" he asked.

"Why doesnt matter, you had countless bitches? Matter fact why am I even explaining myself," I said, hanging up blocking that number also.

IT WAS FUNNY TO ME, now that I have completely washed my hands with Gio, he wanted to call, text, and pop up at my job. But when we were together, I could barely get him to acknowledge me, let alone text or call me. I went back to working on my clients. Kyron was going to be the last one because he had so much going on. He had this battery charge that he would have to go to court for, an album about to come out and a tour where he would be an opening act for a couple big name artists.

I was still trying to see when I wanted to give my resignation. I knew once I did it, they would try to take all my clients that I had. I wanted to make sure that I did it the right way but no matter how it was done, they would try to come after me. Kyron had about two months left on his contract with the company and I knew that if I left, he would follow. My communication with all my clients was AI, but I wasn't sure if they would follow me though.

When I woke up the next morning, I didn't even realize that I had fallen asleep. If it wasn't for my alarm, I probably would've overslept. I got out the bed and went downstairs to start my coffee maker, and turn on the TV to see what the weather would be like. As I sat down on the island, Mico called me to remind me of some appointments that I had today.

"Good Morning, Mico," I said.

"Good Morning. I was calling to remind you of your appointment with Dr. Chance at one. Also, you are meeting with your new clients today; Honey is their name."

"Oh yeah, I completely forgot I took that group on. What time is their appointment?" I asked.

"They will be here at three," he replied.

"Gotcha. Any messages?"

"Yes, the promoter called about Smoove's listening party and making a couple appearances," he replied.

'Okay, I'll call them back when I get into the office. I should be there after my appointment," I replied.

I made me something to eat and poured myself a cup of coffee when I realized that I hadn't heard from Karter. I was tempted to text him, but I figured that he was busy with the girls and getting them settle with going back to school after yesterday. After cleaning up the kitchen, I went upstairs to put on my running clothes so I could do my mile run before I headed to my appointment. I tied my hair up and laced up my sneakers and out the door I went with my head-phones on. I turned my phone on do not disturb so that I couldn't take any calls until I could finish my run.

It took me a good thirty minutes to finish and make it back to the house. I went into the house, started the shower and stripped out of my clothes.

"Alexa, play Drip Too Hard by Lil Baby."

As the music played, I stepped into that shower, and I rapped along.

You can get the biggest Chanel bag in the store if you want it
I gave 'em the drip, they sucked it up, I got 'em on it
I bought a new Patek, I had the watch, so I two-toned 'em

Takin' these drugs, I'm gon' be up until the morning
That ain't your car, you just a leaser, you don't own it

As I was rapping, I stopped because I thought I heard something but when I didn't hear it again, I went back to rapping.

If I'm in the club, I got that fire when I'm performin'
The backend just came in, in all hundreds
Vibes galore, cute shit, they all on us
I'm from Atlanta where young niggas run shit
I know they hatin' on me, but I don't read comments
Whenever I tell her to come, she comin'
Whenever it's smoke, we ain't runnin'

I turned the water off, stepped out of the shower, grabbed my towel and walked in my room to find Karter sitting on my pillows bobbing his head to the music.

"What in the hell are you doing here? How did you get in?" I asked.

"I came to check on you and you left the door unlocked," he replied.

"Oh shit, I guess I did," I replied, walking to my dresser.

"You blocked me or something?" he asked.

"NO, why would you ask me that?"

"When I went to call you, it went straight to voicemail."

"When I go for a run, I turn my phone on do not disturb," I replied, walking to my phone.

"Oh ok, that's why I came over here to see what was up."

"I'm okay, just about to get my day started and go to some appointments," I replied.

"The girls asked me was you my girlfriend," he said.

"And what did you tell them?" I asked.

"I told them not at the moment."

I walked into my closet and pulled out a red skirt that had a zipper the length of the skirt with a lace blouse and a black blazer that I paired with some gold accessories and black Louboutin's. Karter was still sitting on the bed with his shoes off now.

"You know I'm about to leave for work, right?" I asked.

"Yeah, I see you. I'll lock up when I leave," he replied.

"How will you lock up when you have no keys?"

"I have my ways," he replied.

As I CONTINUED to get dressed, he turned the TV on and started to get undress. Then he jumped back into the bed and flipped the channel to Sports Center. Once I was finished getting dressed, I pretended to be looking for something, thinking that he would get the hint that I was ready to leave and get ready also, but he didn't.

"Well, I'm about to leave."

"Ight, call me when you finish with your appointments. You need something?" he questioned.

"Nope, I'm good," I said.

As I turned to walk out the door, he stopped me.

"Hey! Where you going without giving me a kiss?" he asked.

"Oh, I didn't know we were doing that."

I walked over and gave him a quick peck on the lips, which turned into him grabbing me and pulling me down on the bed. As bad as I wanted to allow him to strip me naked and lay in the bed with him all day, I knew I had appointments that I couldn't miss. I grabbed my things again and headed out of the door for a second time.

I jumped into my Benz truck, backed out of my garage and headed to my doctor's appointment. Messing with Karter, I had a good twenty minutes to get there. I arrived at the doctor's office with a good three minutes to spare. I took the time to check myself out in mirror because I felt like my lip gloss was messed up thanks to Karter. I got out, walked into the office and signed in then waited for my name to be called.

I pulled out my phone to check my emails when I felt someone was staring at me. When I looked up, I noticed the lady behind the desk was staring at me, talking to someone on the phone. I paid it no mind and continued to look through my emails then it dawned on me where I knew her face from. She was with Karter's wife the night we ran into them at the restaurant.

One of the other nurses called my name and I went to the back to do my urine test, which was something I was used to on my annual visit. Once I was finished, I went into the exam room, undressed and waited for the doctor to arrive. It took the doctor about ten minutes before she came in.

"Kashmir, here for our yearly exam?" She asked.

"Yes, ma'am. You know I have to keep everything it tiptop shape," I replied.

"Yes, it's a must," she replied, looking down at my chart.

As she was looking at my chart, one of the nurses walked into the room and handed her a piece of paper. The doctor looked at the paper for a minute and looked at me.

"Kash, have you been using protection or your birth control?" she asked.

Shit! I knew I was forgetting something in the morning.

"I haven't been taking them now that I think about it. I have had a lot going on," I said.

"Well, it's too early to tell but it looks like you are pregnant," she replied.

"Wait what? You're kidding?" I said.

"No, I'm not kidding. Your HCG levels are at a fifty, which is the early stages of a pregnancy."

"Oh this can't be happening to me," I replied.

"Are you okay?" Dr. Chance asked.

"Yes, I'll be fine. Let's finish the appointment, I have a couple more appointments after this," I replied.

The rest of the time at my appointment was a blur. I don't remember talking to the doctor let alone making a follow-up appointment for two weeks. As I drove to the office, I didn't know if I wanted to shout for joy or bust out in tears. Here I was on top of my game with my business affairs, but my private life was a complete mess. Now here I was pregnant by a man and we haven't even established a title yet.

I put my best game face on as I walked into the office. Mico was waiting for me and for some reason I got sick to my stomach. I rushed past him and ran to my bathroom. I made it just in time to release everything that I had on my stomach. Once I finished, I brushed my teeth, threw some water on my face and stepped out of the bathroom to find Mico waiting for me.

"You okay, boss lady?"

"Yeah, just an upset stomach," I replied.

"I'll go get you a ginger ale and some saltines."

Coming back into the office, he placed the crackers, a glass with some ice and the soda down.

"Has Honey arrived?" I asked.

"They just walked in. Shanna's taking them to the conference room."

Gulping some of the soda down and eating a few crackers, I straightened out my clothes and headed into the conference room. I wanted to get this meeting over with so that I can take my ass home after I drop off these papers to the bank.

In the meeting, I basically gave the group the run down on how I work. I told them that I wanted to do a test run before I have them sign a contract and it doesn't work out. I went over a number of issues the group had which included fighting, social media beefs, and other issues with the law. Once the meeting was completed, I was packing my things when Karter called me. I sent him to voicemail because at the moment I didn't want to talk to him while I was in the office.

As I was walking back out of the office, Karter called me again. This time I answered his call as I walked to my car. As I was walking, I saw out the corner of my eye, a car approaching but that wasn't new because it was a parking lot.

"Karter, hold on. Let me get in the car," I said.

"Ight," he replied.

The next thing I felt was the car striking me and I went screaming and flying in the air. I landed on the hot concrete hitting my head. After that everything went BLACK!!!

TO BE CONTINUED...

COMING 10/12!

CPSIA information can be obtained
at www.ICGtesting.com
Printed in the USA
LVHW041945061120
670968LV00003B/487